THE THAW

THE THAW

STORIES BY

ÓLAFUR GUNNARSSON

newamericanpress

Milwaukee, Wis. • Urbana, Ill.

newamericanpress

www.NewAmericanPress.com

© 2014 by Ólafur Gunnarsson

Printed in the United States of America

ISBN 978-0-9849439-6-8

Cover design © Liz Green

Interior layout by Nicole Weber

Originally published in Icelandic under the title *Meistaraverkið*, © 2011 by Ólafur Gunnarsson and Forlagið Publishing House, Reykjavik. All stories translated by Ólafur Gunnarsson and Steven Meyers except for "Gaga," translated by David McDuff. This edition published with the generous cooperation and support of Forlagið Publishing House and the Icelandic Literature Center.

For ordering information, please contact:

Ingram Book Group

One Ingram Blvd.

La Vergne, TN 37086

(800) 937-8000

orders@ingrambook.com

❖ CONTENTS ❖

✦ ALIEN ✦

I T SHOULD HAVE BEEN A WARNING SIGN TO HIM, WHAT HER boyfriend had said to her at the café, those six years ago in Paris. They had been sitting outside at Le Select, and her boyfriend had really been chewing her out. "You are so stupid," he'd said, and she'd tried to protest in a feeble, shaking voice. "So stupid. I can't understand why I'm still with you. You stupid, stupid bitch."

He had kept his cool, in love with her already by then, but it should have served as a warning—first, in the way her boyfriend had vehemently described her, and second, how she had just accepted it.

And when he now sat opposite one of their twin daughters and recognized in her features the terrible beauty of his former wife, he was filled with what he thought was anger but could better be described as malice.

They were eating their breakfast. He was getting ready to go to work and drive the daughter to school. It was Monday morning. A gray, harsh dawn smothered the apartment complex. The sad cars were parked in endless rows in front of the houses.

His daughter ate the same way her mother had done, with a closed mouth, her cheeks working at the cereal in a manner he adored.

He pictured his former wife now, after her boyfriend had dressed her down, walking in the hot air of Paris, barefoot on the sidewalk, destroyed by the comment that she was stupid, the reason for her spiritual annihilation. Her boyfriend was supposed to be an important intellectual, a famous writer. But his name, when casually brought up in later conversations, did not ring as many bells as it should have.

The man took up with the woman there and then that evening in Paris and loved her desperately from that day forward. She moved in with him and soon became pregnant. She had twins, two beautiful daughters. After three years she left him for another man who was not in the intellectual game at all, an ordinary Joe who ran a lumber company of some sort.

And she had not only left him, the father of her twins, but she had also left her daughters, when she went to live with the new man. She had left all her belongings too.

Her daughters, her three-year-old daughters! She had walked out on them. What kind of a woman would do a thing like that? It was beyond his comprehension.

The other twin had gone to visit her mother for a couple of weeks.

That left the father and the remaining twin with a lot of unexpected time together; prior to this, the girls had taken care of each other. For a week now they'd been watching videos. He hadn't realized before what an extraordinary number of films the girls had seen.

The previous night they'd watched an old film directed by Ridley Scott. The film was called Alien. It was about a spaceship on a rescue mission that was tricked into coming down to an alien planet so that one of the crew members could become host to a hideous creature that later burst out of his stomach and in no time at all became a monster the size of an elephant.

The girl belched now just as John Hurt, the actor, had done in the movie a moment before the alien tore out of his stomach, and this seemed to remind her of the film. "Did you like the movie we saw last night, Daddy?" she inquired.

"I thought it was very good," her father replied. "I just hadn't realized you girls had seen such terribly scary movies by yourselves."

"Oh, we do it all the time," his daughter said.

"Were you scared by anything in the movie?"

"The alien was scary," the daughter replied. "But not so much the third time around. When I saw the film last night I was most scared for the lady."

"But she got on board the shuttle and managed to save herself," the man said.

"Yeah, but you've forgotten that the alien knew this was going to happen and crept into the shuttle, so it didn't do her any good to blow up the mother ship."

"But eventually she got rid of him for good," the man said.

"Served him right, too," his daughter said.

"Did you know that I'm from outer space?" the man said.

"No," his daughter said, smiling. "You're joking. You're not from outer space."

"It's true," the man said. "I just look like a human but I was sent here years ago from another planet. I'm an alien. And if you saw me in my true form you'd be really scared because I look even more terrifying than the alien in the movie."

"I don't believe you," his daughter said, and she laughed.

The man grew even more insistent at the sound of her laughter. "Well, you better. It's true! And do you know what? Today is my last day on earth." He looked at the clock in the kitchen. "Just after I drop you off at school I'm going to be picked up by the spaceship."

His daughter was looking at him in silence. "Well, it's time now," the man said. "Got to get going."

He rose and picked up the two plates, and noticed that his daughter had not finished her breakfast. "Would you like to finish up?"

She shook her head. She was staring at him.

"Well, let's get a move on," he said. "We don't want to be late for school."

In the car, she said, "You were joking, Daddy, weren't you?"

"No, I wasn't," the man said. He was having a hard time seeing through the windshield. It had begun to snow heavily and the wipers couldn't keep up with the snow.

"Of course you're not an alien," the girl said. "You're just being funny."

"Oh, I assure you I'm not 'being funny.' "

"I love you, Daddy," she said.

They came to the school and the man kissed the girl on the cheek. "Well, this is it," he said. "The final good-bye. I'm already late. I have a rendezvous out of town where I'll be picked up."

The girl opened the door and got out.

As the man was about to drive away, he saw her standing alone on the sidewalk looking at him. Because the door was closed he didn't hear her voice. Her mouth was open in a silent scream of terror.

A WAR STORY

IF THERE WAS ANYTHING POSITIVE ABOUT THE WHOLE AFFAIR IT was mainly the fact that whoever had gotten his daughter pregnant, it wasn't one of the American GIs. It was one of the members of the jazz band that now entertained the soldiers downtown. The boy, strange child that he was, had actually been conceived well before the war.

The boy was now seven years old, and he had always been strange. But the previous day, when the man was dining with the family, his grandson had really surpassed himself, making the man uncomfortable. The boy had suddenly looked up from his plate, pointed to the window and said, "I saw a lady in the sky last night!"

"A lady?" his mother asked.

"Yes."

"And was she out in the street?" the grandmother asked.

"No," said the boy. "She was up above the rooftops. In the sky. She was flying."

Then the boy's mother had one of those crazy, explosive fits of laughter that were the hallmark of her temperament. "A lady in the sky! Flying! Now that beats everything!"

"Tell us more about it," the grandmother said.

The man felt a sudden irritation. Anything out of the ordinary made him uneasy, and his grandson was most certainly out of the ordinary.

"Well," said the boy, "the lady was very beautiful and she was all dressed in blue and holding a yellow harp and she was looking at me. She stood still in the sky for a long time. Her enormously long gown moved in the wind. It moved softly," he added. "And then I just went back to bed."

"Oh, she'd just come down from the Almighty to tell you that you're going to be a great musician like your father," was the mother's response. "That's why she was holding a harp." She was still laughing, but the laughter now verged on hysteria. "Oh, what a funny boy you are," she gasped.

"No, I don't think that's why it was," the boy said solemnly. "I don't like it when you try to make me play instruments. I like drawing better. I thought you knew that."

By now the boy's grandfather had picked up the newspaper. He was trying to read something but couldn't find his glasses—he patted his breast pocket, but the glasses were not there in their usual place.

"But what were you doing up in the middle of the night?" the grandmother asked. "Did you need to go to the toilet, maybe?" She had infinite love and patience for the boy.

The boy looked at his grandfather. "No, I was just very sorry because I'd gotten butter on the wallpaper and wanted to see if the mark had gone away."

"Well, that explains it," the grandfather said, greatly relieved.

The previous day the grandfather had papered the living room walls. The new wallpaper had strange designs that seemed, however, to reveal a regular pattern, and while the boy had been admiring this he had, quite by accident, put a spot on the wall and been scolded for doing so.

"You only woke up because you felt sorry about the spot, and you dreamed it all," the grandfather said.

"No, I didn't!" the boy shouted, suddenly becoming very excited. There was an edge to his voice, something close to outrage. "There was definitely a lady there."

"Okay, you're right," the boy's mother said. "Let's not talk about it anymore."

"Are you taking him to school tomorrow?" the grandmother asked.

"No," the boy's mother said. "I have business to see to."

The grandfather abandoned the newspaper, looked at them all, and before he could be drawn in to whatever it was they were planning, said, "I'm off to work."

"It's all right, dear," the grandmother said to the boy. "I'll take you."

"Okay," the boy said nervously. "It's a big day and I don't want to go all by myself."

The grandfather was out on the porch now and missed the rest of the conversation. He took a look at his car and felt a sense of relief at returning to the normal world. He was a taxi driver, and was duly proud of his car. It was a 1940 Chevrolet sedan.

- 2 -

THE MAN WOKE UP AT NOON. THE HOUSE WAS STILL. HE HAD BEEN working until the early hours of the morning but nothing much had happened—no drunken soldiers, no desperate girls craving the company of their army boyfriends, who were confined to barracks.

The man lay quietly for a moment and listened for any sounds in the house. It was completely still, except for the occasional rumbling of an engine when a car drove past. He called out for his wife in the dark, commanding tone that usually brought her into the room. It was her custom to give him his morning coffee in bed, but there was no reply; she must have gone out on some errand.

Suddenly the door opened and his grandson came in. The boy just stood there staring at him as if he had come across a stranger in his grandfather's bed. "Yes," the man said at last. "What do you want?" The boy had a way of looking at him sometimes that made him uneasy.

"Grandmother said you should take me downtown to school," the boy said.

"She said what?" the man exclaimed. He had never in his life set foot in the place.

"To see the exhibition," the boy replied.

"What are you trying to say?" the man asked. He immediately assumed that there must be some serious misunderstanding.

"Grandmother had to go out," the boy said. "Her friend became ill all of a sudden. You have to take me downtown, for the exhibition. It's today."

The man felt himself getting irritated. "What exhibition are you talking about? What's happening? Where is your mother?"

"The exhibition of the best drawings and paintings by this year's students opens today. My drawing is the very best of them all," the boy said with no obvious pride, as though he took his superiority for granted. Then he looked at his watch. "It starts at one o'clock," he said. "And we mustn't be late."

His grandfather felt uncomfortable. He was not used to dealing with things like this. He drove a taxi, and by doing so provided for the family, but all this business of teachers, authority and too much education made him unsure of himself. He only felt at home in his taxi—there he was in total control of his surroundings.

The boy looked at him with no expression.

"And where is your mother?" the man asked again.

"She went out last night with her friend and hasn't come home yet," the boy said.

The man got out of bed. He felt that he shouldn't inquire into these matters any further, at least not for the present. He got into his trousers and pulled up the suspenders. His feet found his slippers and he made his way to the kitchen. He would have to do without coffee this morning. He had no clue as to how to go about making himself a cup.

The clock on the wall showed twenty minutes to one and the boy was looking downcast and nervous.

"And did your grandmother say when she'd be back?" the man asked. The boy shook his head and his grandfather gave up all hope of escape. "Well, get dressed then," he said. "We'd best get this over with."

He found his shirt, jacket and a tie and put on his shoes. The boy was waiting for him out on the balcony. He looked unusually pale and distracted. "So, what are you so uptight about?" his grandfather asked.

"It's my drawing. I've never taken part in an exhibition before, so naturally I'm nervous about showing my work in public for the first time."

His grandfather suddenly felt an urge to laugh. How strange his grandson was. He was almost like a grownup locked into the body of a child. "Well, don't you worry about it," he said. "I'm sure the other kids aren't as handy with the crayons as you are."

"Oh, they aren't," the boy said looking at him. His face broke into an enormous smile. "I know I'm by far the best."

"Now, how do you know that?" his grandfather asked, feeling his mood change from amusement to sudden irritation.

"I just do," the boy said.

When the school came into view, the man saw that flags were snapping in the wind high atop the pools to each side of the entrance. The steps to the doorway were long and wide and reminded him of the entrance to some official building in Germany he had recently seen in a picture in the newspaper. He felt his old sense of discomfort becoming more intense. Students were streaming through the gate with their parents or other relatives, brothers and sisters. The boy and his grandfather walked up the steps.

They walked slowly along the corridor and then made a tour of all the rooms. The walls were covered with the kind of drawings that children do. There were houses and people and animals—horses and dogs and cats and chickens—in drawing after drawing, with an eternal sun shining over most of the scenery and the people and the animals and the occasional flower. When they had made the rounds, the grandfather said, "Well?"

"Mine isn't here. They haven't hung it up."

"So much for your lady in the sky," his grandfather remarked. "Never pay any attention to dreams; for the most part they're nonsense."

He knew his words were harsh, but he was hoping the whole thing would teach the boy a lesson.

Suddenly the boy looked over to a handsome young man with jet-black hair and a square jaw. "That's my teacher," he said in a low voice. He tugged at his grandfather's sleeve. "Let's go and talk to him."

"Do you think that's a good idea? If they didn't see fit to exhibit your picture, and they sure didn't, you'd better just accept it," the old man said.

But the boy was insistent. He tore himself free from his grandfather and went up to his teacher. Suddenly he seemed even more firm and more independent than usual. The teacher was talking to an elderly couple, clearly trying to hide the fact that he was a little annoyed at the intrusion, but the boy kept on talking. The grandfather felt it his duty to go closer in case his grandson needed any help.

The teacher looked in his direction and said, "We only hung the pictures we thought were good enough to exhibit."

"Come on," the grandfather said. "I'll treat you to a soda on the way home."

He glanced down at the child. The boy looked stunned, as though for the first time in his life he had had a glimpse of reality.

It was a good lesson, his grandfather thought. But he felt annoyed that the child's drawing had not been considered good enough to be included in the exhibition.

- 3 -

IT WAS EVENING AND THE GRANDMOTHER AND THE MOTHER WERE home, but the boy was in bed. He had been in bed, facing the wall, ever since returning from the exhibition.

"How is he?" the grandfather asked in a low voice. He was getting ready to go to work.

As his wife was about to reply, the phone rang. She cupped the receiver with her hand and said to her husband with both respect and a touch of alarm in her voice, "It's the night-duty doctor."

The man took the phone. The doctor needed a taxi for the whole of the evening and the entire night. His regular driver had become ill. The man took a pen and wrote down the doctor's address. "You haven't seen my glasses?" the man asked his wife as he took the piece of paper, folded it and put it in his pocket.

"No," said his wife, "and we gave the whole apartment a thorough cleaning yesterday."

On his way to the doctor's, two enormous aircraft came flying in low over the city to land. They were B-17s. He was able to identify them from an illustrated article he had read in the newspaper. It was obvious that some sort of airlift was under way. It was nearing dusk.

He knew the doctor slightly, had driven him on previous occasions. The doctor was a rather short-tempered man. Influenza was ravaging Reykjavík. They drove from house to house. "Will you come with me into the next house to phone the hospital and write down the patients' addresses?" the doctor asked. "It's all I can manage to deal with these kids and those crazy grandmothers. The grandmothers are the worst; they make more trouble than the children do," he added, stroking his large, bald head.

The man had thought to mention his grandson's strange malady, but now thought better of it. "I'm sorry," he said. "I can't see well enough to write. I lost my glasses last week and can't find them anywhere."

The doctor muttered something and went into the next house. Yet another B-17 came sailing over the town.

It was well after midnight before the doctor got a break from his house calls. The man mentioned the big aircraft to the doctor, who was suddenly filled with an urge to see them. They drove towards the airport.

A few military policemen were guarding the great planes, which were even larger in the darkness. Under their wings the soldiers looked tiny.

One of the MPs, holding a gun, came over to the car. The doctor rolled down his window. He had been educated in America and explained their business. He and the soldier had a short, pleasant conversation. The doctor had been in Idaho and the soldier happened to come from the same state.

The soldier pointed to the sky. Another Flying Fortress was coming in. They could see the warbird growing bigger all the time, and the lights on the wingtips blinking.

Then without warning the soldier ran away from the car. It was obvious that something was very wrong. The plane was coming in over the city lake at much too low an altitude. "My God, it's going to crash-land!" the doctor said.

And like a black goose that had been shot, the enormous plane crash-landed on the gravel airfield. Soldiers ran towards it. The doctor and the man got out of the car. The soldier who had been talking to the doctor was beckoning to them. The doctor returned to the car to get his bag and then ran towards the soldier. The man followed. The broken plane seemed to hiss with anger at its own destruction. Then suddenly fire broke out in the cockpit. The man could see the crew trapped inside. It was obvious from the terror on their faces that they had no chance of escaping. The fire grew more intense with each swiftly passing second. Then, in less than an instant, a fireball engulfed the B-17. Only the tip of the cockpit protruded from the flames.

"Those men are trapped," the man said out loud. "Those men are trapped!" he repeated.

They heard strange crackling sounds, like someone setting off fireworks. "My God," the doctor exclaimed, "they're shooting the crew!"

At the edge of the light cast over the airfield by the fire, the man watched as a group of riflemen, resembling an execution squad, fired at the cockpit, which had now been completely swallowed by the flames. He didn't know if the sound they could hear was the gunshots or the windows cracking from the heat. An officer was pointing to the man and the doctor and shouting something in an angry voice.

"Let's get the hell out of here now," the doctor said, and both men ran to the car. When they were driving away, the man saw in the mirror that they were not being followed. Nothing was visible of the plane now but flames. They met two cars heading towards the airfield, obviously curious. A few men were also running in that direction. "They'll be turned away," the doctor said.

"We were lucky they didn't shoot us," the man said.

"Well, they know who we are, or who I am. I wouldn't be surprised if we're called in tomorrow by the police for an investigation of some sort. They'll want to keep the shooting from getting into the papers."

"They couldn't have done anything else," the man said.

The doctor nodded. "Just take me home. I have to rest a bit. Then I'll phone the hospital and take my own car in the morning to attend to any patients who might phone during the night. You go home now and have yourself a rest, old pal." He patted the man on the knee in a brotherly fashion. "This is quite enough for one night."

They parted, and the man drove home. The shock of seeing the plane's crew being shot like that to save them from suffering had not yet sunk in.

He parked his car and opened the door of the apartment building where he lived. He entered his apartment, took off his clothes in the living room, and looked up into the dark sky, where the boy had seen the angel or whatever it was, but there was nothing to see except the moon, which hung there large and cold. On the sofa the boy was peacefully asleep in his usual way, with his face turned away from the wall.

The man opened the door to his bedroom, slipped under the sheets and lay there perfectly still. He decided not to wake his wife. No matter how hard he tried, he couldn't sleep. Gray light began to show in the window. It would soon be daybreak. He must have slept, because he woke up. He had had a strange dream, or was it a vision? He had seen his glasses. They lay by a fence in front of a house by the city lake, covered by the grass. A few days earlier he had stood there while waiting for someone who had ordered a taxi. "Damn it," he said. He tried to lie still but knew he wouldn't be able to go back to sleep without making sure whether the vision was true. He slipped out of bed.

"Are you going somewhere?" his wife said in a sleepy voice.

"Yes," the man said. "I have to check on something."

"Will you be long?"

"No, I'll be home in time for coffee."

He quickly put on his clothes, went outside and started his car. He drove downtown. He found the fence he had seen in his dream, and the fence pole at the street corner. He stopped the car and got out. He moved the grass near the pole with his shoe. There were his glasses. He picked them up and put them on. They were definitely his.

When he got home, his coffee was ready. As his wife poured him a cup she said, "Oh yeah, the boy's teacher phoned last night. He was rather upset. He said he just wanted to let us know why he hadn't included our grandson's work in the school exhibition. He said that the drawing had been totally unacceptable by any standards, so he'd destroyed it to prevent it causing any more offense. What's wrong with the lad? What did he do?"

"He created a masterpiece, apparently," the man said.

❖ THE THAW ❖

THE BROTHERS WERE HANDYMEN WHO TOOK ON ALL KINDS OF odd jobs. Ragnar, the older one, was a balding, scrawny man in his fifties who suffered from rheumatism, and it showed in the way he carried himself. Jonas, the younger one, had been subjected to his brother's tyranny ever since he could remember, and although he had recently celebrated his fortieth birthday he was nevertheless still the younger brother and would always remain so.

The Second World War had recently ended and the brothers had stopped working for the Americans. They were now building a summerhouse by a lake for a rich importer of all kinds of goods—such importers had prospered in the war's aftermath. Ragnar was the self-appointed foreman and was doing the carpeting, while he had given his brother the job of digging a ditch intended as drainage for the sink and the toilet. The water was taken from a spring on the grassy slope at the foot of the mountain, which resembled an old tooth fallen from the mouth of a horse. Jonas was at it with a shovel and a pick and suddenly Ragnar heard his brother's eager shouts, and when he looked towards him he saw him standing there holding a human skull. Ragnar's automatic response was: "What the hell have you gotten us into now?"

"Gotten us into!" repeated Jonas, dismayed. "I was just digging here when suddenly this skull was sitting on top of my shovel. I haven't gotten us into anything!"

Ragnar dropped his hammer—he had been nailing a sheet of corrugated iron onto a wall—and walked to his brother, who handed him the skull. "It's obviously old," he said, examining it. "Probably the skull of some damn settler. These old Vikings were buried with a lot of fanfare, often in full armor with their shield and sword and a dead horse to ride into eternity, and even a slave girl who was killed and laid in the grave alongside them to give them some comfort in the hereafter, the horny bastards," he said, and he looked into the eyes of the skull and there was a hint of lust and envy in his expression. He reminded Jonas of something he had once seen in a movie, but he couldn't remember which one.

"Well, what should we do now?" Jonas asked.

"Try to think for once in your life," his brother replied. "What would you have us do?"

"Call the proper authorities," Jonas said.

Ragnar looked around as if he was hoping to find someone to share this foolishness with.

"No," he said with an intolerant smile, "that's the last thing we're going to do. You know why?"

Jonas shook his head.

"Because then we're out of a job, you fool. Calling the authorities would mean that all further work on this site would stop while a group of archaeologists take over the digging. At the rate those guys dig at least two years would go by before we'd be allowed to do any more work here. Do I always have to do all the thinking for the both of us?"

"Well, what would you have us do then? Take the skull home?"

"No, I certainly don't want to take that skull home and have to spend my nights fighting the ghost of some damn Viking. You take the skull farther up the mountainside and give it its second burial, and bury any more bones you might come across in the same place. However, if you find a sword or some coins or things like that, notify me at once because that's quite another story." Ragnar appeared to think for a while, then he laid the skull in the grass and ordered Jonas to get out of the ditch, and he jumped down and started digging like a madman, throwing dirt out of the ditch this way and that, with his mind on the imagined valuables, but after a few hectic moments he gave up.

Jonas took the skull and walked farther up the mountainside. He found a good spot to dig and when he had buried the skull he sat down in the grass and surveyed the lake that lay below glittering in the sun. Seabirds were scurrying to and fro on the cliffs above him. On the left shore of the lake there were still some barracks standing, left by the U.S. Army, but most of what had belonged to the occupation forces—radios, tableware, tools, and so on—had been buried in "mass graves" dug for the purpose. It was a real shame, he thought. He looked down at the summerhouse. He couldn't see his brother. Then he turned his attention to the lake, and suddenly a story his father had told when Jonas was young came to his mind.

Each autumn the farmers gathered at the lake to sort out the sheep driven down from the mountains, and once, in 1912—his father remembered the exact year, the same year the Titanic sank—one of them drowned while trying to ride his horse straight across the lake. It had been a bet of some kind. The other farmers warned the arguing pair that it was a mountain lake and that the water was too cold. But the rider, drunk, angry or insane with pride or whatever it was, mounted his horse—the eyes of the terrified animal seeking help in vain from the bystanders—and went straight into the water. The rider and the horse rode to the middle of the lake and then dropped out of sight. Jonas now found himself wondering if there were any remains still to be found at the bottom of the lake. Suddenly a gust of wind from the north sailed across the mountain behind him and swept through the grass all the way down to the summerhouse they were building, disappeared for a while as it passed over the house and then became visible as a small tornado of dust when it went over the road, then reappeared on the lake as a dark path of whirling water. Jonas was aroused from his thoughts by the shouts of his brother.

He rose from where he'd been sitting and walked down the mountainside. It was Saturday and his steps were light—he had bought himself a bottle the day before and was planning to go to a dance in the evening.

Since they had finished for the day, they took their tools inside the house and locked up. While driving around the lake in the direction of town, Ragnar too suddenly remembered their father's story and began to relate it to his brother.

Jonas groaned inside with boredom since he had just been going over the whole thing in his mind a few minutes earlier. He tried to stop his brother by hinting that he knew the story inside out, but it was no use. He wondered why this was a common thing with humanity: you indicated you had heard a joke forty times yet you had to go through the pain of hearing it yet again.

However, Ragnar added a new element to the story that Jonas did not remember having heard before. The whole thing had been because of some woman. Two drunken louts had been trying to impress the same girl and one of them had gone to extremes and wanted to prove his manhood by doing that which everyone else feared—riding all the way across the lake. "Well, he drowned himself, the damn fool, and the girl was a whore anyway," said Ragnar.

"Yeah," Jonas muttered. "Some men go to extreme lengths to hold on to their lady friends." He had stopped listening to his brother telling the old story in boring detail. He focused his mind on the bottle of genever he had bought the day before. It was strong liquor distilled in Holland and it made his mouth water just to think of it—he grew red in the face from the desire to be intoxicated and his eyes grew misty. But then he found his mind going back to the tale, and why he had never been able to hold on to a woman himself. He wasn't a virgin, far from it, but he just seemed to not have any luck with the ladies. His brother had always maintained that this was due to his personality. "You have good looks but that's not enough. When you open your trap and start to talk, your personality—you, Jonas—comes out, and that's when they pack their things and say good-bye." He felt a sudden pang of desperation and helplessness. If Ragnar was right, he was doomed to live alone for all eternity.

The brothers lived alone in a house they had inherited from their parents. The house was small, made of timber and clad with corrugated iron, and painted red with a black roof. By now Jonas was almost panting with longing for the liquor. His brother parked the pickup trunk in front of the old garage that stood next to the house, its two wing doors sagging and leaning against each other. The garage was filled with all kinds of junk. The brothers went inside.

The house had never smelled the same since their mother died—somehow it was never clean enough no matter how much effort they put into it. "Mama would never have left the dishes undone," said Ragnar when they came into the kitchen. If it had been any other day, Jonas would have felt a sudden resentment at this—why was it always his task to do the dishes?—but since he had the bottle waiting for him, safely stored away in a brown bag on a shelf in the closet in his bedroom, he declined to get into an argument. He just put the tap in the sink and let hot water run into it and went into the room and got his bottle of genever. When he came back into the kitchen, he found his brother sitting by the table reading the evening paper. Ragnar turned his back to him and moved his shoulders in a jerky fashion—he had been an alcoholic, though sober for ten years now, and these strange movements of his scrawny frame were the price he had to pay. Jonas got a clean glass from the cupboard, poured himself a stiff drink, and drank it in one go; it went down tearing at his insides, but the warm explosion went at once from his stomach to his head. He turned off the hot water and moved the tab to the other side of the sink, which was split into two halves, and turned the cold water on. He began doing the dishes and he let the water run while he began to prepare himself another drink. His brother ruffled the pages of his paper in the meantime and grudgingly mumbled something about the evils of drink, but Jonas did not hear him—he was much too happy. He made the second drink with half cold water; it was different from the first, the aftertaste somehow a bit stronger despite the water.

When he had done the dishes he put some sausages and potatoes on the burner and had his third drink while the food got ready. The third one was a strong one and it gave him a bit of a sick feeling, but he knew that would pass. While they were eating his brother said, "A woman would do this house a lot of good."

"I'm going into town tonight to try to tackle that problem," said Jonas with the gaiety the alcohol had given him.

"Won't do you much good," his brother said.

"Yeah, I know," Jonas replied, and having gained courage from the drink he said, "as soon as I open my mouth my boring self comes out."

When he had cleaned up after dinner and had his fourth drink, which was now tasting milder, he was happily intoxicated. He took a shower and then got dressed in his best suit and headed for the center of town. It was early but the dance halls would open soon. He had mixed genever and water into a bottle that had once held a pint of Johnny Walker. At the end of the street stood the grassy hill that held the statue of the first settler on top of it and he sat on the bench beneath the dignified Viking and drank in small mouthfuls from the mixture, which had now turned lukewarm. His mood had changed from one of joy to mourning. He was familiar with this from previous experience; a few more drinks and he would be okay again. This thing of gulping down as much as he could before going into the dance hall and buying booze at the bar was just something he did to save himself some hard-earned money.

The evening was a still one with the sounds of the city, cars driving, people calling, children playing, everywhere around him in the distance. The sea lay perfectly calm around the entire coastline and its surface was turning black in the evening sun. And as luck would have it, an old prostitute, a toothless whore, had to sit down on the bench beside him with her sad wino friend. The wino was swearing that he would fuck her before the evening was over and the whore was cursing him and telling him to watch his language. The wino asked Jonas for a drink and Jonas gave him what was left in his bottle and headed for town. He could hear the couple haggling over the drink behind him as he walked down the slope.

The clock in the old cathedral said half past nine as he entered the Hotel Borg. A jazz band was playing and the place had a strange air of adventure about it when compared to the drabness of the town. He sat down at a table and ordered himself a double of what he had been drinking before, and while he waited he took a look around. Not all that many people had arrived yet. A fat, drunken man with black hair smeared with some kind of lotion was teetering desperately from table to table, staring at those present with eyes grown enormous behind thick horn-rimmed glasses. A few young men within Jonas's earshot had a chat with the guy and pointed him in the direction of a lonely-looking older woman dressed in black who was sitting in a corner. The jazz band was blasting the same old program they'd played while the war was still on and the army was in town.

When Jonas turned his attention away from the young men, he discovered that a woman with an amazingly pale face rimmed by red hair had sat herself opposite him. "Do you mind?" she asked. "I usually sit at this table."

"No, not at all," Jonas said, remembering his brother's advice not to talk too much in the presence of ladies.

"You're not really the talkative type," the woman said after some silence. "What's your line of work?"

It suddenly occurred to Jonas that the skull would make an interesting and unusual topic of conversation.

He told the story of the skull more or less as it had happened. He expected that the woman—who had the unusual combination of red hair and blue eyes—would suggest that the authorities be alerted but to his surprise she suggested brusquely that the skull should be used for an ashtray.

"You can't be serious!" he said, laughing.

"I am, indeed. The eye sockets would be great cigarette holders."

"You're quite a lady," he replied.

"You don't know the half of it," she said, and she picked up a black handbag and took out a cigarette.

Jonas waved over a waiter and offered her a drink. He ordered more of the same and she had a double rum. He was full to bursting with what he felt was crazy talk and was having a hard time keeping control of himself.

"So what do you do?" he asked. "You married? You have any children?"

"Do I look like a married woman?" she said, her face showing boredom. "I'm a shop assistant," she added.

The place was now full of people and all of the tables were more or less occupied. The band was going full throttle and sometimes the couples on the dance floor hit the table or an empty chair, causing Jonas and the woman to grab hold of their drinks. "I have a child, a boy. He's six years old," she said.

"Oh, that's nice," he said sincerely. "I like children." He wasn't putting on an act to impress her; he really did like children.

Suddenly, a carpenter whose name escaped Jonas—they had worked together building barracks for the U.S. Army—plopped himself down on the chair beside Jonas and hung his head in a sullen manner. He came to with a start, threw an arm over Jonas's shoulder and shook him hard in a brotherly way, but was unable to utter a word. Then he looked across the table at the red-haired woman and his eyes seemed to lighten and his mind to focus enough to be able to form a coherent sentence:

"It's nice to see you sitting here with one of the loose woman of the town. I'm sorry that the war is over, honey, and that the soldiers have gone? Now you have just us ill-mannered, average Icelandic blokes to spread your legs for."

"Stop talking like that. The lady's with me," Jonas said, and then he grabbed his fellow carpenter by the shoulder and insisted he apologize, but the guy simply fell into a drunken stupor again and hung his head.

Jonas looked at the woman. She had lit a new cigarette and her expression hadn't changed, but she was getting ready to leave the table.

"Now, don't go anywhere," Jonas said to her, and then he rose and lifted the intruder up by the armpits. The intruder got to his feet reluctantly and Jonas pushed him into the crowd on the dance floor. Then he returned to his seat. The woman looked angry.

"What's the name of your boy?" he asked. Her expression warmed a bit. He seemed to have a way with this woman in spite of his dumb self.

"Harald," she said. "Why do you want to know?"

"Children interest me," he said. "When I have money I sometimes buy sweets for the children in the neighborhood."

She nodded disinterestedly. He felt he was losing her.

He thought once again of his brother's words, that when he opened his mouth his true self came out, so he decided to keep quiet. He could, however, feel a nagging desperation growing.

"What that man said wasn't true," she finally commented, holding a cigarette in a dignified manner. He was having trouble making out what she was saying because of the noise of the drunken people and the blasting of the band so he went and sat down next to her and she repeated what she'd said.

He began to tell her another story about a man he knew who'd married a woman who'd had two children, one by each of the occupying forces, a boy by a British soldier and another boy by an American after the U.S. forces relieved the British. And he made both of those children his and now they have two of their own, both girls. To Jonas's surprise, the sentimental tale brought tears to the woman's eyes. "What's your name?" he asked.

"Hilda," she said.

"Hilda and Harald," he said. "That's nice."

"Want to dance?" she asked.

"I'm not much good at it," he said. "I'd rather not."

"Oh, nonsense," she said. "I'll show you how," and there was no denying her. Before he knew it he was on the dance floor stepping on her feet and making a fool of himself. He could feel how thin she was around the waist and he sensed rather than felt what a magnificent figure she had.

They returned to the table but it had been taken by two men and their girls.

"This is our table," Hilda said.

"Not anymore," one of the men said, and the two girls and the other man all looked in the Jonas's direction.

"Screw it," said Jonas, and then he leaned in for their drinks and asked the girl sitting close to the wall to find Hilda's handbag on the floor.

"No, I don't think we should be treated this way," Hilda said. "We're sitting here. This is our table!"

"It's not important," said Jonas, reaching out his hand for her bag. "We're having such a wonderful time. Don't let these people ruin it. Let's dance some more or just go to another bar or café. Come on, please. Don't leave me. I like you."

She nodded reluctantly and he fought his way through the crowd with his lady friend in front of him. She met some girl she knew and stopped to talk a bit and he got their coats while they were talking and then waited patiently like a gentleman until she was ready to follow him outside.

It was a relief to get some fresh air and they walked a bit and he felt comfortably drunk and yet in full control of himself. "What bar do you want to go to?" she asked.

"I don't know," he replied. He was thinking of his brother and whether or not it was a good idea to bring her home.

"Why don't we go to my apartment," she said, "and I'll make you a cup of coffee?"

"That's a good idea," he replied. His heart picked up a beat.

"There's a taxi," she said, waving to a passing car. The car stopped and waited for them.

Jonas walked over to the taxi and opened the door. Hilda got in and gave the driver the address. She lived in the basement of a small house on the eastern edge of town. There was a kitchen, a living room and a bedroom, and she put a finger over her mouth to hush him once they had entered and went into the bedroom and brought the child into the living room. Jonas sat down on a chair in the kitchen to take of his shoes and she came and sat down astride him and they made love like that and then a second time in the bedroom a short while later and then a third time in the morning. "You have to leave before the child wakes up," she said, and then she nudged him and got angry when he was about to fall asleep again.

He kissed her on the forehead when he was about to leave and said, "I'll come visit you at your shop next week."

"Yeah, yeah, that's what they all say," she replied, pushing him out the door.

He felt a bit hungover on his way home and the cool air from the sea had a heavy smell to it and did nothing to retrieve him. He took out his key and tried to enter the house as quietly as possible so as not to wake his brother, but Ragnar was already up and was reading the morning paper. "Hungover?" he asked.

"Hungover and happy," was the other's reply. Jonas took a drink before he went to bed and slept through the day until the smell from his brother's cooking woke him in the evening. They always had something tasty on Sunday. This time it was lamb chops. He evaded his brother's questions as to where he had been, only saying that he had met a woman.

During the following week and well into the next, the work at the summerhouse continued. Jonas dug and laid out the sewage system without finding any further human remains. When that was over he helped his brother with the corrugated iron. The owner came twice that week, the first time to conduct an inspection after the sheets of iron had been hung on the house. The owner was very unhappy about the work. They had put the nails here and there instead of in a straight line and the owner said that it showed sloppy workmanship; he thought he had hired professionals. But he hadn't, and in fact he knew he hadn't; the brothers were just handymen who worked for half the pay. But Ragnar could not very well point that out so he turned to Jonas and scolded him in front of the man and said it was all really Jonas's fault. Then he turned to Jonas and said, "How many times have I told you the correct way to handle work of this kind, boy?"

Jonas said nothing. He couldn't imagine what would happen if he tried to defend himself. When the owner had left, however, Jonas said in a rare fit of rage, "Now, why did you have to go and do that for? It was your fault as well as mine."

"Because otherwise we wouldn't have gotten paid," Ragnar said. "Someone had to take the blame."

The owner arrived the following day with cans of paint. He had calmed down. Jonas had not gone to see Hilda all that week.

He worked up his nerve and took the pickup and drove over there on Thursday. She was genuinely surprised to see him and invited him in. The boy was standing by her side the whole time, tugging at his mother's dress in a jealous manner and complaining about one thing or another.

"You know what," Jonas said to the boy. "I'm a carpenter. I'll make

41

you a real gun out of wood. How would you like that?"

"Real guns aren't made of wood," the boy said.

But Jonas had gotten his attention. "I'll make you one of iron then," he said. "I'm a handyman. I can build things out of iron as well as wood."

The boy had stopped complaining to his mother and was studying Jonas. "Really?" he said.

"Yes, really," Jonas replied.

"Now run out to play," Hilda said to her son.

Jonas invited her to go to the cinema the following evening.

The movie was an American one about a war veteran's homecoming. Life had been pretty wild back home when the boys were abroad fighting the Krauts and the Japs, and the veteran's girlfriend had seen her share of the action. They went to a dance and someone said just as much and the whole scene reminded Jonas of the evening at Hotel Borg. The film had a happy ending—the veteran invited the girl to meet his mother and then they got married at the local church.

Jonas and Hilda had a coffee when the film was over, and Jonas said, "I would like you to meet my brother. Would you come over to our house for dinner on Sunday?"

Jonas was more than a little nervous when he told his brother that he was having a guest over for Sunday dinner.

"Which guest?" Ragnar asked.

"A lady friend," replied Jonas.

"A lady friend," Ragnar repeated, almost outraged, and a dark shade of envy passed over his eyes.

She arrived with the boy a little before noon. She was dressed in her finest, with a big black hat, and the boy was dressed like a little sailor. When he saw the woman, Ragnar behaved like he had some kind of a shock, and Jonas assumed this was due to envy. The boy reminded Jonas about the gun he was supposed to make for him but his mother told her son firmly to be silent.

"It's okay," Jonas said. "We'll build you a gun any day now."

They were having breaded lamb chops with rhubarb jam and potatoes from the brothers' own garden—there was a garden in front of the house where it was sunny, and a single rowan tree appeared to stand guard over it. None of the children in the neighborhood dared steel potatoes from the brothers or take a rhubarb stalk to munch on. If you did so you were as good as dead, or so it was said.

Jonas noted with pleasure that Hilda was discreetly checking out the house. He couldn't understand his brother's displeasure though—Ragnar ate in silence and jerked his shoulders back and forth more noticeably than usual. Jonas attributed this to his brother's jealousy.

When Jonas drove mother and son home late in the afternoon, the boy brought up the subject of the gun again. "Don't worry, brother," Jonas said. "I'll get to work on it soon."

And he did so that afternoon. He had a workbench in the garage and welding tools he had acquired when the U.S. Army left, and he made a machine gun from various odds and ends and was most pleased with the results, so he was confident the gun would please the boy. His brother only scoffed when Jonas showed him the gun. "I've seen this woman someplace before," Ragnar said.

"If you're referring to the fact that she had her son by an American soldier, I'm very well aware of that," replied Jonas.

"And what do you want with this woman?"

"To get her to live with me, hopefully," Jonas replied. His brother scoffed again. Jonas was surprised that Ragnar didn't ask him where he intended to live with her. He knew his brother so well that this made him uneasy.

They were putting finishing touches on the interior of the summerhouse all of the following week. The owner's wife had planted a few trees to shield the house from the wind that constantly blew from the east, but it would be years until the trees were big enough to give the hoped-for result.

One evening in the middle of the week, Jonas took the gift to the boy, who was delighted. While the boy ran out to show off the gift to his playmates in the neighborhood, Jonas nervously brought up the subject of whether Hilda would be willing to consider helping him and his brother out with household work. The house, he said, had somehow not smelled right since his mother died.

"You want me to come live with you, is that it?" she asked.

"Yes," he replied. To his own surprise he grew hot in the face.

She moved in the following week with her son and her few things. She didn't have any good furniture to speak of except for a giant cupboard they put by the wall in the living room. It had belonged to her grandmother and had great sentimental value. What was left of the furniture they stored in the garage for the time being. Her income added to that of the home and she was an excellent cook. The boy slept in the living room—unfortunately Ragnar was at home most evenings. Jonas felt uncomfortable making love to Hilda when his brother was within earshot. His close relationship with the boy grew closer with each passing day. On the weekends they'd take walks down to the harbor and Jonas would buy the boy a hot dog. Sunday, for the two of them, became "hot dog day."

One Sunday when they came home he found Hilda extremely upset at the kitchen table—she was shaking and crying, her hair wet with sweat—and when Jonas asked her what had happened, the boy following all of this grown-up stuff with great fear and concern for his mother, Hilda told him that Ragnar had been coming on to her. "I want to leave," she said.

"Your old apartment is rented out," he said, "and anyway we were going to get married before Christmas."

"You'll have to tell your brother to never ever do this again," she said.

"I will," he said.

But she felt his equivocation. "If you don't, I'm leaving with my son," she replied. "I'll not have him be a witness to this."

"I will," he said again.

He did it the next morning while he and his brother were driving to work. The atmosphere had been tense while they were getting dressed and Hilda had stayed in bed until they were gone.

"But she's a whore," Ragnar said, shocked. "It's not only that she had a child by an American. She was one of their girls. She's a whore and she's making a fool of you! What would it matter if I did it with her or not?"

Jonas was in such emotional turmoil that he was unable to speak. When they drove down the gravel road to the lake he was glad that it was the last week of work at the summerhouse. "You leave her alone or else," he was able to say at last to his brother.

"Or else what?" Ragnar replied.

Jonas didn't answer, but when their lunch break came he took the keys of the car, drove around the lake and asked the foreman of the group, who was working on cleaning up after the army, for work. Jonas was hired on the spot. He said he would be able to start work the following Monday.

Ragnar had found them some work in town, and they were to begin that same Monday. He was quite upset when he heard that Jonas wouldn't be joining him. "Have you gone mad?" he said. "Has the whore taken control of you? Robbed you of all your senses?"

"Don't you call her that," Jonas said in a quiet voice.

There was a strained atmosphere during the evening meal, with the boy eating with downcast eyes and Hilda shooting fierce looks now and then at the brothers. She refused to sit, and ate standing. Later in the evening, however, when they were about to go to sleep, she sat on the bed in a way that reminded Jonas of a little girl. She was taking some pills and drinking a glass of water, so sadly deserted in the world. She had a hard time swallowing.

"What is it, darling?" He touched her shoulder.

She moved her shoulder to avoid his touch.

He went to the window and looked out at the naked tree, stripped of leaves. Autumn had now set in with unusually hard frosts. But that was nothing compared to the atmosphere in the house. On top of it all, Ragnar was having a hard time finding a new partner and that made his mood even worse. He was grumbling at the food Hilda cooked. "I'll be moving as soon as I can find an apartment," she said one evening after she and Jonas had gotten in bed.

Jonas rolled on his side and looked into the darkness in desperation. The cold outside persisted—even the sea was frozen solid.

Since the shop where Hilda worked was in the opposite direction of the boy's school, it fell to Jonas to take him to school in the morning. The boy had taken to calling him Papa. "I'm afraid, Papa," the boy said when Jonas was about to drop him off one morning.

"There's nothing to be afraid of," Jonas replied. "You're as strong as the other boys. Just go show them."

"It's not that," the boy said. "I'm afraid for you and mother."

Jonas went to work. He had won the argument with his brother over the pickup and had gained some confidence in his own courage. They were doing their final cleaning up by the lake. Only the foundations of the barracks were still standing. On this particular day they were given an absurd job. The waste left by the army was truly extraordinary— deep ditches were dug to bury truckloads of usable things, both tools and household stuff, radios and things that could have been easily sold or given away—but the job for the day was one of the stupidest Jonas had ever witnessed: they were told to drive about thirty trucks and jeeps onto the frozen lake, where the vehicles were meant to sit until a thaw came and the ice melted. The cars were started, driven onto the middle of the ice and then the keys handed over to the foreman. It was an astonishing sight to see all the trucks and jeeps in the middle of the lake with the soft, powdery snow blowing around them.

In the evening, as Jonas told the tale, Ragnar shook his head and spoke of the immense waste, and Hilda agreed. The boy was so excited about the whole thing that he had a hard time going to sleep and would speak of nothing else until Jonas promised he would take him the following Sunday to show him the sight.

"Why don't we just take one of them home?" the boy asked. "We could hide it in the garage."

"We could take some parts from some of them," Jonas replied. "A lot has already been removed. But it wouldn't do any good to take a whole car. We could never register it. Everyone would know where it came from. It's such a small town we live in," he added.

"It's too small," the boy replied. Jonas didn't know what the boy meant and a voice inside him told him not to ask.

That evening's meal was fresh haddock. Jonas and the boy were late and Hilda and Ragnar had been arguing. "He wants me out of the house," she said as soon as the two of them came through the door.

"It's my house as well as his, and you're welcome to stay," Jonas replied, and then he watched his brother's face become contorted.

"Our mother used to run this household!" Ragnar spat out. "Have you completely forgotten that?"

When the meal was on the table, Ragnar took a piece of fish and put it on his plate, but when he touched it it wouldn't separate from the bone, since Hilda in her overwrought state had removed it uncooked from the boiling water. It was half raw. It was as if all the aggression that had been mounting within the older brother for months exploded at this moment. His scrawny figure shot up from the table and he grabbed hold of the woman and starting beating her unmercifully across the shoulders, his arm stretched out like a sledgehammer, while he shouted, "I'm not used to this! I'm not used to this!"

The boy screamed in terror and tugged at Jonas, who, unable to move, merely watched what was happening in a disbelieving stupor. When at last he moved to intervene, his brother rushed to the door, grabbed his coat and slammed the door on his heels.

"You let him do this to me while you just sit and watch?" she screamed at him.

"I was on my way to help," he said. He felt sick inside because of the boy.

The boy ran to his mother. "We're leaving now," she said to her son. "I'll spend the night with a friend of mine. You're the weakest person I've ever met in my life."

"I'm going to kill him," he replied.

She gave a forced, hollow laugh.

He was no more able to stop her leaving with her son than he had been in preventing his brother from giving her a beating.

The brothers were not on speaking terms in the days that followed; the mood in the house didn't match that of the weather, as a thaw had set in. Each day, Jonas went to the shop to speak to Hilda but she would have nothing to do with him. "What if we get our own apartment?" he asked.

"Neither I nor my son respect you anymore," she replied. She invited him to the back of the shop and he thought she wanted to tell him a secret, but what she wanted to show him were her bare shoulders, black and bruised.

It had been a week since the brothers had spoken to each other, and Saturday and Sunday went by in stony silence, which felt unbearable to Jonas, so he added to his own disgrace and said, "It'll be a sight to see when the ice melts and the cars sink."

"Yes, why don't we go out there tomorrow morning," Ragnar said, relieved to hear a human voice. "They just said on the radio that it would rain tonight."

The next day they went to look at the cars. The lake came into view. The cars sat in the middle of the lake as if a deserting platoon had left them there after a fierce battle. "Let's stand protected by the summerhouse," Ragnar said. "We can watch from there. The wind, as always, is blowing hard from the east."

Ragnar parked by the summerhouse and the brothers got out and looked at the lake. They stood in silence. Suddenly Jonas picked up a beam of wood from a pile of leftover timber and hit his brother hard on the neck. Ragnar fell to the ground. He was still conscious but the next blow took care of that. Jonas lifted his brother up with all the strength his hatred gave him and carried him onto the lake. Water was floating there in pools even though no cracks had yet appeared. He sat him behind the wheel of one of the trucks. Then he took the box of pills the woman had left on her night table; there were three pills left, which he forced down his brother's throat, and then he made him swallow the pills by pouring some vodka into his mouth from a flask in his coat pocket. Ragnar was not in the habit of taking sleeping pills and would sleep until darkness set in.

Then Jonas drove back to town.

Ragnar slept, lying face forward on the steering wheel of the truck. He didn't see the first drops of rain as they hit the hood or the black skies that rolled in over the mountains from the east and the heavy rain that came with them. The thaw had set in with a heat like that at the height of summer. He didn't see the cracks that shot away from the group of cars in all directions when the ice began to break up.

By then he had begun to sober up a bit from effects of the sleeping pills, enough to dream. He dreamed about the lake. He was riding a horse in the middle of it. The shore was not very far away. To his surprise, his long-dead father was standing there. He felt very happy to see him and was certain that this time the horse would make it all the way to the other side.

❖ THE BEAUTY CONTEST ❖

- 1 -

SIGVALDI TOOK THE ELEVATOR DOWN FROM THE ELEVENTH FLOOR at Austurbrún 4, where he owned a small apartment. That morning a newspaper reporter had paid him a visit because of that coming evening, and it was the same old routine: "When did you first start singing with a band?" "Didn't you guys almost make it in England?" Sigvaldi thought he could discern a slightly suppressed smile in the corner of the man's mouth. How many times had he been forced to listen to this question? Another question, however, was new to him, and a bit malicious: "Young people today don't have the faintest idea who you are. How does it feel to be a relative unknown performing tonight with a world-famous singer?"

"It feels good," Sigvaldi said, successfully concealing his irritation.

"What are you doing now?" the reporter asked.

"I'm an independent employment agent."

"What kind of services do you employ?"

"I run a cleaning service," Sigvaldi replied.

He looked at himself in the mirror in the elevator. His long hair was turning gray, there were bags under his eyes and his face was marked considerably by age. His career had declined severely in recent years and now he had almost stopped doing gigs. In the sixties he had sung with some of the most popular groups in the country and often stood on the stage of the Laugardalshöll arena with thousands of people screaming in front of him. When he was the singer for the Local Cats they had opened up for The Hollies.

The elevator door opened and he walked out of the building's entrance. His old white van stood frozen solid in its parking place, a thin film of ice on the windows. He started it up and dug out a scraper from beneath the driver's seat and cleaned the windows. Then he drove in direction of the Hotel Reykjavík.

Sigvaldi parked a good distance from the hotel. On the rusty body of the van was painted in large letters: CLEANERS INCORPORATED. The hotel was having its grand opening that night, with a concert and a beauty contest. He would be appearing at the event as a representative of the sixties. The name of the hotel had been neatly displayed in big blue letters on the roof above the main entrance. Scaffolding rose to the west of the entrance; the exterior of the hotel was still in need of finishing touches. Sigvaldi cleared his throat, swept his hand lightly through his hair at the temples, held his chin high and walked through the front door. In his mind was a steady beat: I'm on my way to meet the one and only Rod Stewart! I'm going to meet Rod Stewart!

Sigvaldi nodded to the doorman and asked, "Is Grjóni in yet?" He asked in order to ensure that the doorman wouldn't begin to inquire who he was. This had happened quite a few times of late, in particular with younger people. It was clear that the news reporter had told the truth. Nobody knew who he was anymore. By calling Sigurjón, the hotel manager, by his nickname, Grjóni, Sigvaldi could at least indicate that he had once been a part of the in crowd.

The doorman nodded and Sigvaldi walked past the coat check and looked into the ballroom, where several tables covered in white tablecloth were distributed across the floor and an elevated, horseshoe-shaped stage rose on the opposite side of the room. Waiters were setting the tables. Otherwise the ballroom was empty. Sigvaldi was somewhat absentminded. It was as if the fact that he would be meeting Rod Stewart at any moment had him in a stranglehold. He walked across the shiny tile floor and up onto the stage and then went backstage. There were four large rooms backstage full of astonishing girls trying on dresses, having makeup applied, whispering nervously to one another and occasionally breaking into laughter—the beauty contest was about to begin.

"Have you seen Grjóni?" Sigvaldi asked cheerfully.

One of the girls, who had a thin elfin figure, long snakelike golden locks and a small chin, looked at him with inquiring eyes. "Who?"

"Sigurjón...Grjóni?"

"Yeah, he was here just a moment ago."

"He went upstairs somewhere," a makeup woman said without even looking at Sigvaldi. She was taking care of a black-haired beauty who watched her every move in the mirror, her face like a pale white mask.

"He's going over this evening's program with Rod Stewart," said the girl with the snakelike locks.

"Hmm, I wouldn't mind…," someone said.

"Well, it could happen. He has a room right here in the hotel."

"But he only wants blondes."

"Girls, don't be like that," said the one with the snakelike locks. "I have a boyfriend."

"So what!"

"Then Grjóni's in his element. The good old manager chatting with the entertainer, that's where he's at his best," said Sigvaldi to himself, feeling a bit out of place.

Suddenly the dark-haired one with the waxen face looked up from the mirror. "Hey, aren't you a singer or something?" she asked with a cheerful voice, her eyes lighting up.

"Hell yeah," Sigvaldi answered.

"Didn't you sing with the Local Cats in the old days?"

Sigvaldi didn't deny it.

"I found your record buried under some junk out in the garage the other day and my dad found a record player so I could listen to it. I have to say, I thought the music was fantastic! I think it should be available on CD."

"Yeah, I totally agree," the makeup woman said, looking at Sigvaldi, who now realized that she was about the same age as he was. "The Local

Cats are a group that won't easily be forgotten."

"No. And besides, we went to England back then and were something of a success," Sigvaldi said.

Contrary to what he had expected, these words didn't generate any interest. He stood for a moment enveloped in fleeting memories of bygone days. They had gone to London and played at the Crawdaddy Club, they had signed a record contract and world fame seemed to be right around the corner, an article from Melody Maker had been translated into Icelandic and distributed in the press back home, and everybody thought they were on the verge of making it when the song "Soul on Ice" launched to number forty-eight on the charts within the first week of being released, which seemed remarkable to the band's British manager. They waited with bated breath, but then the song went down a spot within a week before dropping off the charts entirely. They decided to persevere, playing a few gigs here and there, but after three weeks the drummer gave up and flew home.

A face suddenly appeared in Sigvaldi's mind, that of a black prostitute he had picked up in a narrow alley; he had been so stoned at the time that he wasn't even sure he had been with her at all. Why did it all have to end like that? The Local Cats were the best group in the country, ever, yes, the best group in Scandinavia and beyond— the whole thing came alive right there and then. It felt as if the group was waiting onstage once again ready to fill the house with its unique sound, but each and every one of them had parted ways a long time ago: one was now a carpenter; another ran a supermarket; and Villi, the drummer, was dead. Sigvaldi was the only one who had stuck it out and stumbled on in the business.

"Hi, Sigvaldi!" He looked up and saw Sigurjón Magnus Svavarsson, aka Grjóni, the hotel's manager and former band manager, waving at him, and Sigvaldi smiled and waved back. He felt that he was overly eager and that his smile was more like a grimace. Right beside Grjóni stood Rod Stewart himself. Rod was wearing a light green suit and his blond hair was cropped and spiked, jutting into the air. He was shorter than Sigvaldi had imagined and his eyes focused on the girls as soon as he and Grjóni stepped into the makeup room. Grjóni seemed to have no trouble at all relating to Rod, as he had a lot of experience dealing with celebrities. The makeup girl said something to Sigvaldi; he tried to concentrate on what she was saying but was still lost in the clouds. He resented his own awkwardness. I just hope I don't blush, he thought. Oh God, please don't let that happen! Ever since Grjóni had called a fortnight earlier to tell him he would be performing with Rod Stewart, Sigvaldi had repeatedly rehearsed in his mind how he would begin the conversation: "You may not believe it but my band and I once hit the charts in England!"

Sigvaldi discreetly pressed the palm of his left hand against the right one to wipe off the sweat while the other two men moved toward him, as in a bad dream. Grjóni hit him on the shoulder like an old buddy. "It's good that you could come, Sigvaldi, old pal," Grjóni said. Then he turned around and extended his arm to draw the two singers closer together. "This is my friend, Sigvaldi Sigurdsson, a distinguished local talent. Sigvaldi, old chum, allow me to introduce you to one of our role models and mentors. Here's a man who managed to become all we ever dreamed of."

They said their how-do-you-dos looking each other in the eye and Sigvaldi felt he was misery incarnate in the presence of this famous performer. Rod's nose stood like a pillar between his water blue eyes. Word had it that Rod owned a palace in England and played soccer now and then. Someone of his stature who was interested in soccer naturally owned a whole team. If he got bored and felt like going to Los Angeles, he flew by private jet, of course. What was it that I was going to say? Sigvaldi thought, looking at Grjóni and hoping for some help. Sigurjón patted him patronizingly on the shoulder: "This guy once had a song on the charts in England!"

"And what song was that?" Rod Stewart asked.

" 'Soul on Ice.' " Sigvaldi answered.

"Rings a bell," Rod said.

Sigvaldi looked at him, surprised. "Rings a bell!" he repeated.

They stood there together in the silence surrounding them. Grjóni had gone off to talk to the beauty queens. "What do you say, girls? It'll be hard to choose between you. If I was judging, you would all wind up in first place and get the same ribbon: MISS ICELAND 1985."

Sigvaldi smiled at Rod, assuming that Rod was just trying to be courteous. Sigvaldi's smile became more cynical than he intended: "You don't really expect me to believe that you remember my song? It debuted at number forty-eight, held there for a week and then dropped out of sight."

"I remember 'Soul on Ice,' my friend," Rod said. He snapped his fingers and crooned, "I was a soul on ice, yet it seemed like paradise…" He put his foot to the floor to stomp out the beat and Sigvaldi looked with amazement at the pop star, who was actually singing the English version of "Frysikista," which Sigvaldi himself had freely transposed into English. "I tried to get the publishing rights to that song at the time," Rod said. "My manager checked all over the place. I was going to record it, but the rights were hard to track down."

Rod snapped his fingers and launched once again into the first verse: "I was a soul on ice, yet it seemed like paradise…" He looked at Sigvaldi. "That's the way it went, yeah." All of a sudden they started singing together, Sigvaldi Sigurdsson and Rod Stewart, as if they had been doing so for ages, and Rod looked fondly at his new mate until they both hit the last lines of the verse: "You and I were meant to be, is that not plain to see?"

"Yeah, great song!" Rod said eagerly. "I still remember the lyrics. That song truly deserved to be in the top ten, as opposed to all the rubbish that makes it onto the charts these days. It's really quite surprising it didn't do better. If I remember correctly, that song popped up in a conversation I had with Moon, and Moon thought it was terrific!"

"Moon?"

"Yeah, the late Keith Moon of The Who. I loved that guy. A true mate of mine."

Rod launched into another section of "Soul on Ice" and Sigvaldi joined in. He was all of a sudden aware that the girls had gone quiet and that the makeup woman, who had a redhead planted in the seat in front of her, looked at them and smiled, and Grjóni brought his hands together for the two singers, and some of the girls followed suit.

"But that's not all."

"No?"

"Jimmy Page saw you sing in a club in London once and was seriously thinking about talking to you when he was putting Led Zeppelin together and was looking for a singer."

This news struck Sigvaldi like a lightning bolt of such magnitude that even though he heard the words and nodded his head he still didn't quite comprehend what had just been said. Rod Stewart had turned his attention to the girls and was mingling with them, greeting each with a handshake. Most of them took it with a shy smile. Sigvaldi followed Rod through the throng in something similar to a state of shock, feeling stiff and awkward beside him. One of the girls, the skinny one with the golden snakelike locks, greeted Sigvaldi warmly. "My name is Ásta Björt Arngrímsdóttir," the girl said, and he smiled mechanically without taking any notice of the name; it vanished from his mind instantly—he was more upset and off balance than he had realized. At the center of his mind a calm voice kept saying over and over, "I'm standing here talking to Rod Stewart like it's the most natural thing in the world, and Keith...Keith Moon was really impressed with my song, and Jimmy Page, he felt I might be suitable as the singer of Led Zeppelin." He repeated these words to himself full of quiet joy, but regardless of how many times he did so he still couldn't believe it. He couldn't imagine himself being onstage with Led Zeppelin even though he had drunk with them all night long at the club Las Vegas on Grensásvegur after their concert at the Laugardalshöll arena on June 22, 1970. "Bonzo was one crazy son of a bitch," he said out loud.

"What?" asked Ásta Björt Arngrímsdóttir.

"John Henry Bonham, the drummer for Led Zeppelin."

Why hadn't Jimmy Page said anything? Sigvaldi thought, astonished. He hadn't mentioned this when we met. Actually Pagey never said much at all, he usually just murmured indecipherably into his chest. You could hardly drag a single word out of him.

Sigvaldi stood like an idiot in the middle of the floor with his mouth hanging wide open, causing Ásta Björt to exclaim, "What is it?"

Rod Stewart was surrounded by women and was giving one of them his autograph on a napkin.

Sigvaldi came to. "Uh, yeah, I'm always a bit absentminded when I'm about to go onstage."

She looked at him, surprised. "Really? God, I'm surprised to hear that. I assumed it became routine for someone like you. I'm so distracted myself I hardly remember my own name. I have no idea how I allowed Sigurjón Magnús to talk me into this."

"Talk you into what?"

"Participating in this competition."

"Oh, well, I'm not surprised at all," Sigvaldi said. "He talked me into coming here tonight. There isn't a person in the entire country he couldn't talk into doing whatever he wants them to do."

Grjóni suddenly said loud and clear, "Okay, girls, it's time. I'd like to welcome all of you on behalf of the Hotel Reykjavík. Soon I'll go onstage and announce the evening's program to our guests; the house is filling up fast. Now, as you all know, you'll go on first in an evening dress, then in a bikini, and finally in a dress of your own choosing, and then our two stars, the British and the Icelandic one, will sing a few songs and keep the mood going before Serial Killer, the heavy metal band, takes over and entertains our guests after the final results are announced." He looked at his wristwatch. "You've of course met the pageant director and the judges several times already. They're locked in a room upstairs; it was decided they would only see you onstage tonight, so that their judging would remain unbiased."

Grjóni the manager had his shit together and Rod Stewart looked back and forth between Grjóni and the girls with the genial vibe of a man who doesn't understand a word of the native tongue. Sigvaldi stepped out of the makeup room to take a look at the stage. Large red curtains separated the stage from the ballroom and with the cool eyes of a seasoned professional he watched the whole setup. A couple of guys from the band Serial Killer had arrived—these were younger men and he knew nothing about them except for a few things he'd heard through the grapevine. With the dignity of a veteran he nodded to the lead guitarist, who acknowledged Sigvaldi's presence in turn. However the big fat drummer with the bald head apparently didn't give a shit about old, burned-out pop stars.

Sigvaldi peered out into the ballroom. The tables surrounding the horseshoe-shaped stage were nearly full but the TV crew's lights hadn't been pointed toward the stage yet. There were a lot of smartly dressed people there—friends and family members of the beauty queens at the tables in front, other guests farther back—and waiters ran about distributing oven-baked lamb. All of a sudden Sigvaldi was gripped by an old, familiar anxiety, one he thought he had outgrown from being in the music business for so long: My God! he thought. Am I going to demean myself by being nervous tonight? Now he fully realized the impact of the news he had earlier received from Rod Stewart. Jimmy Page had him in mind when he was putting together Led Zeppelin, the greatest rock band in the world. Why hadn't Page contacted him? Wasn't there a door somewhere that you could just slip through and live your life all over again? He felt as if all of his greatest opportunities were behind him now. Life had run its course. He felt enormous sadness.

Suddenly he felt someone yank his jacket, and he turned around. There stood Grjóni. "He wants you to do a song with him," Grjóni said.

"What?" said Sigvaldi, stunned.

"It seems that meeting you was like love at first sight, my man. He wants to do a duet with you on 'Maggie May,' one of his most famous songs. You must know that one?"

"Of course."

"And then he wants to sing 'Soul on Ice' with you."

Sigvaldi stared at Grjóni like an oafish baboon.

"Do you have the lyrics to 'Soul on Ice' on paper? He's a bit rusty on that one."

"Are you nuts? Do you think I carry twenty-year-old lyrics around in my pocket?"

"Then go sit down in the dressing room and jot them down so the man can bring himself up to speed," Sigurjón said, and then he disappeared into the ballroom.

- 2 -

The girls all waited in line at the small door that led to the stage. They stood there grinning nervously, some talking compulsively and breaking into uncontrollable fits of laughter, others keeping their cool, as if the whole thing had nothing to do with them, as if they were someplace else.

Ásta Björt Arngrímsdóttir did not often pray to God, but she now turned her attention to Him: If I win, dear God, I'll donate half of the prize money to the poor. She then took back the promise, not entirely sure she could keep it, and instead asked Jesus to give her strength: Good Lord Jesus, please, I don't want my father, mother, brother or sister to be ashamed of me. She heard the emcee; he must be standing at the front of the stage now. During rehearsal the previous night she had stood there under the floodlights convincing herself not to be startled when she walked out there now. She knew where her mother, father, brother and sister were seated. If she could just keep them at the forefront of her mind, as if she were walking into the living room at home, making sure not to smile too much or awkwardly, then everything would be all right.

The first girl went onstage and Ásta Björt heard a loud voice proclaim, "Linda Björg Bragadóttir!" The stage door gobbled the girls up one by one: "Elva Ýr Ingvarsdóttir!" Fucking bitch, she couldn't stand that girl. She was completely intolerable. Why was this whole thing so frantic? "Why are we so far back in the line?" she asked a brunette standing in front of her. She couldn't for the life of her remember the brunette's name but the girl's face was all covered in red spots. "I think this should have been done in alphabetical order. Then I would have gone on first."

"No," said the other girl, looking irritated. "I would have been ahead of you. My name is Aldís. And they have the nerve to place us at the very end of the line."

"Yes, I understand," said Ásta Björt. "I'm just so confused and absentminded."

"Which isn't a surprise considering how disorganized this whole event has been," said Aldís. "I was all ready to quit at one point."

Then Aldís disappeared onto the stage, swinging her hips to the drumbeat, and Ásta Björt finally got a full view of the stage, where the girls had aligned themselves on a platform in front of the band. Aldís walked back and forth across the stage, wearing a blue dress that generously revealed her back and chest. The dress was designed to emphasize her breasts, of course, but somehow it all came off as really tacky, Ásta Björt thought as she watched Aldís join the line onstage.

And then suddenly she heard the voice of the emcee, as if she wasn't expecting it: "The next contestant is Ásta Björt Arngrímsdóttir. She's nineteen years old, lives in Gardabaer and intends to work as a flight attendant this summer." Ásta Björt felt as if she were nailed to the floor. She was the last one to go on. "Come on, hurry up and get out there," someone behind her whispered. "You look wonderful. You outshine them all!" The one doing the whispering was the sweet old singer with gray-speckled hair. He had moved up behind her without her having noticed. Sigvaldi was his name, wasn't it? He gently squeezed her hand with a warm palm and then she walked onto the stage.

She stepped quickly, swinging her hips, and turned her face to the crowded room. She had adamantly decided to think of something pleasant at this moment to make sure that her smile came from the heart, but she forgot everything she had decided upon and instead made do with the warm pressing of her palm by the older man. The gentle touch of his hand had filled her with warmth and she felt that the smile she sent out to the audience was sincere. She didn't have to lean on her parents for support and the floodlights were brighter than she had anticipated, so bright she couldn't see anyone in the audience, from where the applause seemed to roll down from the ceiling and right over her. She sailed past the emcee to the far end of the stage and then turned around and walked back—it was as if time had come to a halt and yet also flew by so fast. She walked across the stage again and saw the old singer standing to the side of the curtains watching her. She could feel energy flowing from him and she gave him a calm and assured smile. She went back to her place in the line and felt wonderfully relaxed, and then the emcee said, "Ladies and gentlemen, now you have seen the contestants in their evening dresses. Next they'll come out in bathing suits and then finally in dresses of their own choosing, and each of them will give a short heartfelt speech, but between segments the world-famous singer Rod Stewart will"—and at this point a large round of applause erupted—"entertain you and his backup vocals will be provided by none other than our own well-known star from the sixties, those good old days, the one and only rootin'-tootin' son of a gun, Sigvaldi Sigurdsson!" Another wave of generous applause followed Sigvaldi's introduction.

- 3 -

The girls then flocked past Sigvaldi, who thought angrily, the one and only rootin'-tootin' son of a gun? Why in hell did the man have to introduce me in that manner? He had given the lyrics to "Soul on Ice" to Rod Stewart earlier and Rod had sat down at a table backstage to get the lyrics straight in his mind. Sigvaldi had no need to refresh his memory of "Maggie May". He had sung the song more times than he could remember at dances all across the countryside. Why didn't I ever hear from Jimmy Page? he thought, seeing in his mind a stadium full of seventy thousand people, all screaming at Led Zeppelin.

"Let's give the singers a good round of applause," the emcee said. Rod Stewart, in a shiny white suit, walked confidently past Sigvaldi, who followed him into the rousing ovation. Both singers were handed microphones and Rod launched into "Maggie May," the first single he had recorded when he embarked upon his solo career, and the song rolled straight to the top of the charts at the time, making him instantly world famous. Rod took a single long step forward on the stage and his hoarse voice washed through the hall as if a dam had suddenly burst: "Wake up, Maggie, I think I got something to say to you." Sigvaldi followed along nervously, thinking that Rod would hand a few verses over to him, but it soon became clear that Rod intended to keep the song to himself. There was nothing wrong with that, of course, since it was his song, but he should have at least given Sigvaldi a chance, since they were supposed to be singing duets.

He decided to have his say. But then he made the mistake, since he was so taken with his hero, of responding physically to Rod, and the audience laughed—not maliciously, more of a friendly laughter, but laughter still. Sigvaldi raised his voice in desperation, trying to push his way in, but Rod stood his ground and dug into the heart of the song…and then they approached each other—the song was almost over, dammit! I've been performing in this country for thirty years, Sigvaldi thought angrily, and I'm a first-rate Icelandic singer. He had to force himself into the song and through the rest of it Rod had to back off because the Icelandic "nobody" had the stronger voice. The audience thought this was hilarious and broke into laughter. After the two singers had taken a bow, the emcee said, "And now the girls will come out in their bathing suits."

On their way backstage they met the tiptoeing row of girls and Rod pointed his finger at his colleague. "What the hell do you think you're doing, you cunt?" Sigvaldi followed Rod down the hallway in desperation. Had he fucked up the only big industry contact he'd made in the last quarter of a century, and possibly the last real opportunity he would have for the rest of his life? Rod stormed into his dressing room and slammed the door behind him. All of a sudden a large man wearing sunglasses appeared in front of the door, preventing Sigvaldi from entering to make things right again. A security guard! Sigvaldi hadn't noticed him before.

He had to get ahold of Grjóni, who was the only one who could sort this matter out. "Where's Grjóni?" he asked the stagehands, but nobody had any idea what had happened to the hotel manager. He must have gone out into the ballroom.

All the girls were lined up onstage in their bikinis when Sigvaldi emerged into the ballroom. He moved between the tables, scanning the place for any sign of Grjóni. There were a lot of young people in the audience and many of the young men had teased hair in the style of Duran Duran. But there were some older folks too, with children, no doubt relatives of the contestants. Grjóni found Sigvaldi first. "What are you doing wandering about like this?"

"Rod's locked himself in his dressing room!"

"Yeah, have you completely lost your mind? What the hell were you thinking taking his wind like that? Can't you behave yourself without letting your dreams of world fame burst out in such a crazy manner? I thought, Sigvaldi, that because I've done so much for you over the years that you would never stab me in the back this way. Have you any idea what I had to pay to get that man to come here so that I could open the hotel in style. Millions and millions of kronur! And why did I ask for you? It's quite simple: I always want the very best for you!" Sigurjón took a deep breath. He wasn't quite as angry as he was pretending to be. In reality he was in his element. He was a genius at unraveling situations as complicated as this one was. He shot out of the ballroom and Sigvaldi followed on his heels. The security guard moved aside for the hotel manager.

Grjóni stayed inside for a short while and then came out again the very essence of willful determination. He walked straight up to Sigvaldi, who was waiting to hear what had happened. "Okay, he's agreed to do another song, no thanks to you, so now get up on that stage and keep your trap shut except for when I tell you not to. Help the man do this song, your song. This is a great honor for you and you're not going to fuck it up like you fuck up everything you get involved with, whether it be a woman or whatever, and if you make a mess of this evening I will make damn sure that you will not let out as much as one yelp in any godforsaken dancehall in the countryside." Sigurjón stared straight at him and raised his voice: "Sigvaldi, do you understand what I'm saying? It's important that you pound this into your head or else I'm not allowing you back onstage."

While Grjóni was chewing out Sigvaldi, the room filled up with girls. They were getting ready to put on their own evening dresses.

"Sigurjón is always the same, good old Grjóni," Sigvaldi said, smiling at the girls, but then he fell silent when Rod Stewart stepped out of his dressing room. Grjóni took hold of both singers by their elbows and said in English, "Let's leave the girls alone while they get undressed, he he. It's time to tear the house down during the second half." He added in Icelandic, "Remember what I said, Sigvaldi. Keep your ego in check."

Rod and Sigvaldi walked onstage to deafening applause. "I was a soul on ice, yet it seemed like paradise. It's here I was meant to be, is that not plaaa-in to see?"

Rod Stewart blew new life into the old song. Sigvaldi found himself filled with admiration at how it blossomed in Rod's brilliant interpretation. He wondered why he hadn't put more effort into composing in general—maybe he would in the future. He stepped back from the spotlight and let Rod take over. It was easy. He himself was really at center stage. Rod was only doing his version of the song and the audience knew it. Rod sang from the depths of his soul. They owned the room at that very moment, both of them, and it was as if the blinding lights were clapping hands when the enormous applause hit them. Sigvaldi let Rod walk alone to the front of the stage and take a bow. The star applauded the audience and then jumped quickly over to Sigvaldi, took him by the arm and led him to the front of the stage, where they took a bow together. They would have done another song if the girls hadn't been waiting in the wings in their evening dresses ready to say a few words.

The first girl stood center stage dressed in blue, addressing the crowd. "I woke up this morning as the rain thundered on the roof, but when I got up and the sun had already begun to shine, I began to think of all I have been given—my cat, Bjartur, my parents, my sisters and brothers, and my boyfriend, Ernir, who is here this evening. Who am I? I asked myself, but I have no answer except that my name is Íris, I'm nineteen years old, my favorite food is roast beef with baked potato, and yes, my favorite singer was onstage here tonight, Rod Stewart. And what will I do in the future? Well, marry my boyfriend, have children, be a real woman and not let new-age feminists confuse me."

"What's that chick talking about?" Rod asked.

"You're her favorite singer and she wants to steer clear of feminists in the future," Sigvaldi said.

"Thank God, what a beautiful bird." Rod Stewart stomped his foot on the floor, his eyes glued to the stage as the girls came on one by one.

"I love cooking and anything to do with art," a blonde said, her hair ratted, teased, molded into a golden arch cascading all around her shoulders. Rod appeared to be a sucker for blondes since he had his eyes trained on her, enthralled, his mouth slightly open, a lustful look on the horny old goat's face. "I can't think of anything more boring than arguing with people," the girl said. "To be honest, I'm neutral when it comes to politics. I intend to complete my education in graphic design and I'm excited about learning to be a makeup artist for film and theater. I'm going to own a car, a house, children and a husband after I have explored life a bit. And what person would I most like to meet? Why Sean Connery, of course. He's been my favorite actor ever since I was a little girl."

"I'd like to ask you a question," Sigvaldi whispered.

Rod Stewart looked at him, waiting to hear the question.

"Why didn't Jimmy Page ever contact me for an audition if he was so interested?"

"I figure he must have met Robert Plant," Rod replied.

"Look at this one," Grjóni said, draping his arms over their shoulders as Ásta Björt Arngrímsdóttir walked over to the microphone in a long white dress.

- 4 -

Her eyes had adjusted to the lights. She'd listened to the other girls' speeches and had not been very impressed by them. She knew where her family sat although she could not see them. She had planned to say something in a similar vein and had even written some lines down on paper, such as "This summer I will be working as a stewardess for Icelandair," and she had also typed out the words to the poem "Hotel Earth," by Tómas Gudmundsson. She suddenly realized how empty all of it sounded and she thought of her family and started speaking without thinking. "I don't really think it's that important for me to win this competition because what's most valuable and lasting are other people. Good friends, good parents, good sisters mean more than any worldly success. One pressing of a palm, one precious moment of support is worth more than standing in this spotlight. I want to thank everybody who has supported me in this competition; their friendship will remain special to me regardless of what place I end up in. I wish the best to all the girls who have taken part in this beauty contest tonight and I hope they will be at peace with the results, that they do well, and that I too will be at peace with the results, whatever they may be. I would be dishonest if I did not admit that I hope I'll do as well as the other contestants. Whatever the outcome, I hope it won't have a negative effect on the friendships that have developed among us these past few weeks."

She stepped back in line to mild applause. Now, somewhere out there in all the brightness, the judges were trying to come to a conclusion. Ásta Björt looked at the girl standing next to her, who was wearing a dim, slanted smile. Did the other girl feel that Ásta Björt's speech was pretentious? All of a sudden she herself felt that it was, however beautiful the words had sounded. "I really appreciate the friendships that have developed among us these past few weeks." What sentimental crap! They were all jealous of one another, each and every one of them.

Drumsticks pounded on skins, finally the event was coming to an end. Ásta Björt looked forward to going home, locking the door behind her and crawling under a warm blanket. The judges appeared onstage, three women, three men, and the head judge approached the microphone. He said a few words about how difficult the decision was, that seldom or never before had it been so hard to reach a conclusion. Ásta Björt didn't hear any of this because of her pounding heartbeat. The drumsticks danced hypnotically on the cymbals to raise the excitement level then fell into dead silence. "And in third place," the drums danced again as the head judge made the announcement, "Ei-dís Einarsdóttir!"

Eidís stepped forward and received a bouquet of flowers. As Ásta

Björt heard the applause fade she felt a sharp pain in her breast. Her heart was beating so hard, her hearing had become numb and she was racked with fear as she watched the second-place girl step into the spotlight. She had promised herself many times in the weeks leading up to this moment, ever since she was given the chance to take part in this competition and her mother had said, "There's no way you can walk away from this opportunity when all these good folks are ready and able to open the gates of the world to you," ever since it was decided she would take part she had prepared herself for the unexpected, if it so happened that she won she would not clasp her hands to her quivering cheeks and begin to scream with her mouth open or let the tears flow through her fingers. She had occasionally witnessed this happening on television—it was strange that girls made such complete idiots of themselves—but now when she heard her own name called, in first place "Ásta Björt Arngrímsdóttir!!!" she began to shake uncontrollably, she opened her mouth wide to let out a scream of joy because if she had tried to keep it in she would have exploded, and she tried to keep control of herself by raising her hands to her face, but when it became clear to her that she had behaved in the very same manner she feared most she couldn't restrain the tears that suddenly flowed down her cheeks. And she did no better controlling the shaking in her body; she inhaled deeply and blew out air and gasped. They all surrounded her and she was led to the throne and made to sit down between the two girls who had ended up in second and third place, and then she screamed once more without the slightest possibility of holding it back, because she had never, ever really expected to win. Something light and delicate was placed on her head—it was the crown, the golden crown—and she was draped in a white sash. Who put it there?

MISS ICELAND 1985.

And the lights in the ballroom transformed in all sorts of ways, a transparent white wall blinking and dancing across the room as everybody rose to their feet and applauded, a black throng of people, all clapping together in a rhythmic beat. The beauty queen was the only one sitting down in the entire hall. The TV crew had placed itself right in front of her, newspaper reporters waited beneath the stage for a chance to surround her and cameras snapped in rapid fire. "So how do you feel right now?" came the first question. "I'm still just trying to take it all in...it really hasn't registered yet..."

And then Rod Stewart placed a wreath of flowers on her head.

❖ KILLER WHALE ❖

IT WAS SATURDAY AND OLAF WAS LATE. HE HAD DECIDED TO BE ON time so that his ex-wife wouldn't scream at him, but he was late anyway. They had been divorced for three years now. He spent time with his daughter every Saturday, and for the last six months his ex-wife had had a new husband, with whom she and their daughter lived in a big house right downtown. Once when Olaf had forgotten to pick up the child, the ex-wife phoned him later that day from the public library, which didn't prevent her from screaming at the top of her lungs—she was a woman born with the heart of a wolf.

The traffic came to a halt and Olaf looked at his watch and worried. If the early Saturday traffic jam did not dissolve soon, he risked being quite late. He was not good at making plans, or so his ex-wife had always told him. When they had been married she used to write everything down on bits of paper for him: where to go to find the particular vegetables she wanted, which dry cleaner to use, where to shop, and in what order. She would even remind him to go to the post office and check for mail. She numbered all of the places so he would save gas and not spend his time driving from one end of town to the other.

The traffic suddenly began to inch forward but just when he thought he might slip across the intersection the light changed to yellow and then to red again and he was stuck there once again. It was raining a little and he turned on the windshield wipers as his cell phone rang. It was her and she was upset, though not quite at the point of yelling.

"You should have been here by now," she said. "Katharine is excited and she misses you. And she is afraid you might not come!"

"I'm just stuck in heavy traffic," he said. "Bad luck."

"Bad luck, my ass! The traffic is always heavy on Saturday at this time. You know that very well, and you should have taken that into account."

"I'm sorry," he said.

"You are insulting your daughter." She was beginning to raise her voice. He knew that if he objected she would begin screaming. It was their daughter's illness that had slowly destroyed their marriage.

"Learn to plan things," she said sharply. "That's what I was always trying to teach you."

He thought of saying "I'm a slow learner" but managed to restrain himself since that would only provide an opening for an argument, and, besides, just at that very moment, the light switched to green again and the traffic began to move. "I'm on my way," he said, trying to add a friendly tone to his voice. "The jam is loosening up," he lied, but by some miracle it turned out to be the truth. A road to the left was just being opened up again by the city road workers dressed in their fluorescent uniforms and a whole group of cars went that way, clearing the main road for the remainder of the traffic.

"Well, hurry. You know she's getting very excited and she can't be allowed to get excited! She just can't!"

He lowered his cell phone and accelerated as much as he could but, regardless, he could see by the clock in the church tower, which hovered over the city, that he was already ten minutes late.

She lived in an old, sturdy timber house with small windows right down by the city pond in the expensive part of town, and when he finally saw the house in full view he knew he was far later than he should have been. An ambulance was sitting outside the house with two wheels up on the sidewalk. He parked his car across the street and his ex-wife came running down the wooden steps as soon as she saw him.

"Are you insane?" she screamed. "I told you to be on time! You know how much she loves you! She can't tolerate the insecurity of waiting. She's had another attack. And it's a bad one! It's very bad this time! The nurse is with her now. You're lucky she didn't die."

He found himself wondering about that as he hurried up the stairs and entered the house. His ex-wife's new husband, an exceptionally good-looking man who lifted weights and had thick, wavy hair, sat at the table in the parlor wearing an expression of doom. He was a lawyer and he owned the house. Olaf suddenly felt sorry for the guy. He seemed to know his place already. Olaf hurried up the next flight of stairs to the nursery. His daughter was in bed and a young nurse he hadn't seen before was attending to her. The room was spacious and the pond could be seen through a series of rowan trees. He asked the nurse how the girl was doing.

"She's not feeling very well," the nurse replied. "There is a lot of puss in her lungs and I've been helping her to cough it up." The nurse rolled the girl back and forth in the bed and lightly hammered on her back. The girl had a blue shade on her usually pink cheeks. "And she lets me know it. I know when she lifts her legs that she is angry with me. And she is very angry now. Please come closer so she can see you."

Olaf did as he was told and looked into his daughter's eyes. It was as if they were made of silicone; he saw no sign of recognition.

"I have to remove your mask for a moment," the nurse said to Katharine. "Get ready for it."

She removed the oxygen mask. The girl let out a gasp as the nurse rolled her on her side, and a yellowish froth covered her lips. It seemed to Olaf that Katharine was without the oxygen mask for an eternity, which made him think not of heaven but of hell. His daughter was in hell. This is what hell must be.

The nurse put the mask back over his daughter's face, adjusted her limbs here and there, and said, "She's feeling much better. Surprisingly better, as a matter of fact. Were you very close once?"

"We still are," he said.

"I'm so sorry," the nurse said. "A slip of the tongue on my part. I'm truly sorry." The nurse became hot in the face, and when she blew her hair away from her cheek he noticed how pretty she was.

His ex-wife suddenly appeared in the doorway and the nurse turned toward her and then slowly shook her head from side to side. The ex-wife disappeared. It made Olaf happy that someone had such power over his ex-wife.

"It seems that your arrival might be the reason why she suddenly feels so much better," the nursed said. This was almost like some sort of a flattery, and it made him feel awkward. He looked around the room; it was filled with toys his daughter had once been able to play with. A light brown rocking horse on iron springs with a white mane especially caught his attention. He had bought it for her as a Christmas gift five years earlier, almost at the onset of her illness.

"Will you take her to the hospital?" he asked the nurse.

"No, not this time. Her recovery at the sight of you, as I said, was quite remarkable."

"Tomorrow is Sunday," he said to his daughter. "I'll come for you then if your mama says it's okay. I'll talk to her now. She'll come upstairs right after I leave and tell you if it's okay." He suddenly pulled himself together when he felt the nurse staring at him. "I'll come tomorrow regardless! We can't let another week go by."

The girl looked up at him with such loneliness in her otherwise neutral eyes that he felt himself almost on the verge of asking the pretty young lady standing beside him if she would be willing to go to bed with him. It was an insane thought.

He went to the bedroom door and called down to his ex-wife. "Will you please come look after her now!"

Olaf left the house in the company of the nurse. It was almost as if she protected him from his ex-wife when they met her on their way downstairs. "Are there many children in the country with this illness?" he found himself asking, knowing full well the answer, but he couldn't think of anything else to say.

"I think there are about three," she replied.

When they arrived at the bottom of the stairs he said to the husband, who was still sitting at the same place at the parlor table with the same doomed expression. "Would you kindly tell Gudrun I will be back for the girl tomorrow?"

The man nodded with an expression that seemed to say he wished they would all simply vanish. He didn't even rise to accompany them to the door.

The day outside seemed extraordinarily fresh after such a short visit.

"How long do you expect her to live?" Olaf asked as they walked down the outside steps. The ambulance driver was sitting at the wheel speaking into a cell phone about something or other, which, judging by the look on his face, was of a great importance. When he saw the nurse he gestured for her to hurry.

Olaf already knew the answer to his question, and the nurse confirmed it: "She should be dead by now. Children that start to age prematurely in this manner don't usually live this long."

He felt a strong urge again to ask her to sleep with him, but, given the occasion, this feeling was more than shameful. She was about to get into the ambulance when he was inspired by an idea.

"I'm taking my daughter whale watching tomorrow," he said. "Would you perhaps like to accompany us, if you're available? Or maybe you don't work weekends? But it would give me a great feeling of security, in case she has some kind of attack." He blushed, adding, "And I'll pay you, of course."

"I would be absolutely delighted," the nurse said. "And you don't have to give me anything. Do you have a piece of paper and a pen so I can give you my phone number?"

He took out his cell phone. "Go ahead, just tell me." He punched in the digits as she told him her number.

He turned around and sent his ex-wife a knowing smile, goading her, and then the ambulance drove away and he got into his car.

Olaf's car was in fact a van. He had a small furniture business and did most of the upholstering himself. The car was equipped to carry his daughter's wheelchair in the back, so that the two of them could enjoy their moments together. And when he looked at the empty compartment, it made him think that he had some shopping to do. He was sure he wouldn't be taking any unnecessary detours as he drove across town this time. His ex-wife had always been on him about that.

He decided that he would go and buy some black velvet.

He bought all of his upholstery supplies and fabric from and old importer who ran his business out of his home. The importer was nicknamed "the Boxer" because of his flattened nose—the result of having been kicked by a horse when he was young—and had sold fabric to the Olaf's company ever since it was run by Olaf's father.

Olaf parked his van on the street where the Boxer lived and walked the path to his house. Both the sidewalk and the path itself were strewn with leaves. It was autumn now and getting colder. The tourist season was almost over. He would have to check on the whale-watching tours. His daughter's favorite thing to do was to take a boat out into the bay, where the giant animals could be seen rising from the depths to display their massive backs and spout out of their blowholes. This was the only time he really saw life and joy fully rise up in her eyes.

When he came closer to the house, Olaf saw that the Boxer was in the process of working. Through the window he could see his bald head and massive shoulders outlined against the darkness of the cellar. The Boxer looked up but did not greet Olaf; it wasn't his custom to greet people from his desk. He had a strict set of rules. Even his sons, who were now middle-aged men and worked for their father, were used to knocking before entering the office.

Olaf stepped down toward the door, went in to the dark corridor and knocked. "Come in," a voice said.

Olaf entered the office.

"I'm about to close for the day," the Boxer said. "You're late. And don't you know it's Saturday? Why don't you come tomorrow?"

"Because I'm working this weekend," Olaf said. "That's why."

The Boxer looked up, surprised. "Well, that's news to me. And you sound like you're serious about it. I don't remember anyone working weekends in the upholstery business, except for your father."

"Well, I'm a changed man," Olaf said. "Something happened."

The Boxer snorted in contempt. "What is it that you need? As I said, I'm about to close up."

"Black velvet!"

"Black velvet?" the Boxer repeated, staring at him. "Now, what do you want that for? Did someone ask you to upholster a coffin?"

Olaf smiled. "No, nobody asked me for that. They're usually done in red, anyway. An old lady wants to redo her sofa and chairs in black velvet, that's all. Is there anything unusual about that?"

"Yes, in fact, there is. I have some in stock, all right. I've had it in stock for years because nobody's been buying it. But I can see that times are changing."

"Indeed they are," Olaf said.

The Boxer found the keys to the garage, which he used as his storage room, and they headed in that direction. While the old man was fumbling with the lock, he said, "And how is your daughter?"

"Pretty much the same."

The Boxer didn't reply to that but instead said abruptly, "Do you still do that crazy sport of yours?"

"What? No, no, I stopped doing that a long time ago."

"Well, that's good to hear. It always worried your father. He was afraid that you might drown."

"Well, I didn't."

"How is it down there in the deep?"

"It's another world, actually. You forget all about this one."

The Boxer managed to get the door open, interrupting the

conversation. They entered the garage. It was a well-maintained, well-heated place, because of the need to preserve all of the different fabrics that were stored there.

"Black velvet," the Boxer muttered. "The world is going crazy."

"I thought you'd be happy to get rid of it."

"Yes, in fact, I am. How much of the stuff do you need?"

"About fifty square meters."

"That's a lot."

"Its coming into fashion," Olaf said. "And I want to store up."

The Boxer rummaged around in the piles until he found the black velvet. "It's old and it's cheap and it should be just enough for what you need."

"Well, bill me for it, then," Olaf said.

He carried the fabric down to his van. He was a strong man and could manage the load in only one trip.

He phoned the tourist-information center when he got home. Yes, they confirmed, there was a whale-watching tour scheduled for the following day, the last one of the season.

Sunday was bright and sunny even though autumn had fully arrived with clear, brisk air around a faded yellow disk of sun. He phoned the nurse. She told him her address. She seemed to be happy to hear from him. Then he phoned his ex-wife and told her when he would be arriving there: two o'clock sharp. He laid the receiver down before she had time to start an argument.

He picked up the nurse, who when dressed in her regular clothes looked even more beautiful than the previous day. She lived in the eastern part of town and they chatted a bit while he drove to the city pond. He felt awkward, even a little bit in love. They arrived in front of his ex-wife's house at two o'clock sharp. He opened the back of the van so that he and the ex-wife's new husband could lift the wheelchair and his daughter inside. The girl had her breathing mask on but he nevertheless thought he could hear her wheeze in pleasure. He shook the husband's hand. He had never known the fellow to utter a single word. His ex-wife stood there on the veranda looking like a general. When she saw the nurse, she came down to greet her. "When do you think you'll be back?" She addressed the nurse in order to show her contempt for her ex-husband.

"Around five o'clock," Olaf replied nevertheless. "The folks at the whale-watching place said that the trip takes two hours at least." The ex-wife gave him a glance and nodded. Her husband was so pleased when they were leaving that he even shook hands with Olaf again.

Olaf drove toward the harbor. The weather was becoming even more beautiful. He could see that there was snow on the top of the mountain across the bay and for a moment wanted to draw his daughter's attention to it, but then he decided against it because it would require too much effort. And, besides, the nurse was tending to the child tenderly. He liked her more and more all the time.

There was a shop on the street next to the harbor that sold sporting goods: shotguns and ammunition, swimming trunks, gear for scuba diving, footballs, javelins, discuses, running shoes and so on. He parked the car outside it and said to the nurse, "I have to jump into the shop for a moment to get some things. It won't take long." The nurse nodded. He took a look at his daughter, who sat there in her wheelchair like a solemn old woman expressing approval of her well-behaved grandson.

He went inside; the owner of the shop, who Olaf was acquainted with, greeted him with a look of surprise. "Going swimming?" the owner asked. "It's been a while since I've seen you." The owner leaned forward and peered out the window. "And a lady! Congratulations!"

"No, no, not today," Olaf said. "But the autumn weather is simply wonderful. I've been in touch with the guys and a group of us are going to go for a swim in the bay sometime next week. So I'm going to need a can of grease and a new rubber cap, a yellow one, for my head—and please be quick about it. My daughter is outside in the van, waiting. And, for your information, the lady is her nurse."

The owner of the shop said quickly, so as not to get into a discussion about Olaf's daughter, "You guys are nuts, all of you! You should have been born seals!" He handed Olaf the rubber cap and Olaf tested it. It was a bit tight but it would do.

"Sea swimming is one of the healthiest sports you can think of," Olaf said. "It makes a man out of you." He nudged the shoulder of the shop owner.

A gorgeous blond, who was inspecting jogging shoes, looked at the two of them and smiled.

The owner added up the two items on the till and put them both into a shopping bag. "Well, give my best to the guys and be careful not to go too far out," he said. "Watch out for the killer whales—I'm serious."

"Killer whales never attack men except when they're in a pool," Olaf said patronizingly. "And they're only found further to the east."

"I know," the owner replied. "What's the matter with you? Can't you take a joke anymore?"

"I guess not," Olaf said, smiling slightly. "I'm a bit absentminded today. Well, I have to hurry."

He hurried back to the car and the girls. His daughter sat there in the wheelchair with a satisfied look.

They drove down to the waterfront a short distance away. The whale-watching vessel sat at the pier clearly marked on its stern for the benefit of the tourists. The van rattled a bit on the docks. A lady in a black uniform was selling tickets next to the ship. Olaf and the nurse got out of the van. Olaf walked to the rear of the van and he could see the sea black and shimmering with oil beneath the planks. He jumped into the back, untied the wheelchair and rolled it toward the edge; the nurse took hold of the footrests and together they lifted the wheelchair down onto the dock. Olaf's daughter looked up at the sun blissfully.

Olaf rolled the wheelchair to the side of the vessel and paid the lady in black for the tickets. "Will you be needing any help?" the lady asked, looking at the girl in the wheelchair.

Olaf looked up at the steep stairway that led from the dock to the deck of the boat. With its thin wooden rails screwed onto a platform as a substitute for actual steps, the stairway wasn't exactly suited to wheelchairs, but Olaf had seen worse. "No, we'll manage," he said.

He took the handles of the wheelchair and walked backward up toward the deck, with the nurse holding onto the footrests. Once they were onboard Olaf pushed the wheelchair to the rear of the ship. Since the tourist season was coming to a close, there weren't many other whale watchers onboard. He felt comfortable with the nurse and the child, almost as if they were a family.

"You don't know how often I've prayed," he said suddenly.

"Prayed?" she asked curiously.

"Well, perhaps 'prayed' isn't the right word. 'Hoped for a miracle' is maybe a better way of putting it."

"I understand," she said.

He was going to say that she couldn't possibly understand when the engines of the ship suddenly roared, the stairway was removed from the side of the vessel by the staff and there was a sudden movement as the ship set out to sea. It was only a few kilometers to the whaling grounds and Olaf walked to the bow of the ship as the nurse pushed the wheelchair behind him. Other passengers gave them kind-hearted looks. The gray autumnlike expanse of the sea appeared hard as steel. He nodded to an older lady, who said she was from America—Phoenix, Arizona, to be precise. She had long dreamt of visiting Iceland with her husband. She introduced Olaf to the elderly man next to her and then said that it had turned out to be more wonderful than either of them had ever expected but what they had really come to see was the whales. She had heard that there were plenty of them out in the bay. "Yes," Olaf said, feeling a strange sort of pride, as if the whales belonged to him.

He nodded toward his daughter and said, "My daughter loves them."

The American lady said something that he didn't hear, because at that point he noticed there was moisture in his daughter's eyes from the cold breeze. The nurse hadn't seen it so he wiped the tears away with the back of his hand. His daughter's eyes had more life in them now. She knew she was going to see the whales. She looked at him with love. The nurse was looking out over the bow, shading her eyes with her hands, even though the sun was shining on their backs. They continued on for about twenty minutes. Suddenly there was an announcement from the bridge on the loudspeaker: "Whales ahead!"

The sound of the engine decreased and was eventually cut off; the boat slid near to a field of whales that were spouting and snorting and feeding at the surface, in full accord and friendship with man, the onlooker. A whaling ban had now been in effect for a quarter of a century, and when they thought about lifting it they realized that the tourist trade had become more important, so they extended the ban.

"They don't kill them anymore," Olaf said to the American lady, who nodded her head in approval.

He turned to his daughter, took her out of the wheelchair and lifted her up in his arms so she could see. The nurse held on to the oxygen mask. The girl was making delightful sounds of joy. And the herd of whales was snorting and wheezing and blowing so that it all sounded like a symphony. The moment lasted a long time, and then the engines started up again and the boat drove in a circle as if the whales were inside an arena.

When that part was over the engine came alive again at full power; it was time to head home. Olaf put his daughter back into the wheelchair. She was in a state of total bliss. It made the nurse laugh. "I think we've perhaps seen something of the miracle you wished for today," she said.

Olaf smiled slightly but said nothing. For some reason the trip back to the harbor seemed quicker than the trip out. "There weren't any killer whales," the American lady said. "That was a bit of a letdown."

"No, they're loners," Olaf said. "They live in their own herds, by themselves. They don't mix with other whales. They attack them. They feed on them. They're fierce and independent and have no enemies of any kind in the sea. They live by the shore to the east, about three hours from town, but they don't have any whale watching there."

"Oh," the lady said with an odd look in her eyes, and then they took leave of each other.

Olaf waited until all of the other passengers had left the boat. The procedure of getting the wheelchair down the stairway was much the same but now in reverse. Then they rolled the wheelchair to the van.

Olaf drove the nurse home. She said good-bye to his daughter. And then she added when he didn't say anything as she was leaving, "Will I be hearing from you?" Her face flushed a bit.

"Yes," he said, proud and shy. "Yes, you will, definitely. And thank you for asking. You have no idea how much this means to me, especially today."

She looked at him, surprised, and then her face lit up. "Well, I'm glad to hear it, and I certainly look forward to it." She closed the door and he watched her firm, beautiful figure as she walked toward the house.

Then he looked at his daughter. She was sleeping now, exhausted. That was to be expected. He didn't drive her home but took the road that led out of town. When he came to the intersection that led either east or west, he took the road east. He drove for three hours straight while dusk slowly grew and the landscape changed; the mountains became higher the further he drove into the countryside and the cliffs with the many caves up high on their faces turned from brown to black as the sun slowly approached the sea. The sky was getting dark, and clouds darker still were set against it.

He saw it then, the hill down by the seaside and the cliff beside it, with space enough for a ship to be hauled up between them, and indeed this was the place, legend had it, that the first settlers had landed their ships more than eleven-hundred years earlier. The sand on the shore here was as black as a raven for miles around. Olaf drove toward the shore and felt the going becoming heavier when he went off the rough gravel road and onto the sand. Then, lying beneath the hill, with the large rock to his left and the waves braking in front of him, he shut off the engine.

He got out of the car, opened the rear door and took out the black velvet. He threw the fabric over the car to fully cover it. Then he gathered some stones to hold down the edges, took out a shovel and piled sand over the edges all around the car. When this was done he undressed. He had put on his swimming trunks before he left the house in the morning. He took out the jar of grease and covered himself all over. He had waited until the very end to cover up the rear of the car.

He opened the back door and went inside. His daughter was awake so he rolled the wheelchair to the edge of the back compartment, lifted it out and put it onto the sand. Then he took her out of the wheelchair, laid her on the sand and put the wheelchair back into the car. He considered undressing her and covering her with grease to protect her from the cold but then thought better of it. It was not the thought of her red, bloated body that made him change his mind, but mercy. The cold would kill her almost instantly. He took the yellow rubber cap he had bought by the store near the harbor, though, and put it on her head. He took out his old black cap and put it on. Then he covered up the edges of the car at the back so that no wind could get under the sand and tear the fabric off. When winter set in, it would be days, even weeks, before the car was found.

Then he lifted the girl into his arms. There was no expression in her eyes. He kissed her on the forehead. He walked into the breakers and began to swim out to sea with his daughter in his arms. The sun was now a glowing disk of fire on the horizon and flames were jumping out of the sea like molten lead. His daughter's body gave a jolt when it hit the cold water. Then it felt as if she shriveled and got smaller.

He was a good swimmer, used to the sea, and he swam as it slowly got darker and then became pitch black. He knew that she must have been dead from the cold for a long time now. He swam as far out as he could manage but he was feeling very tired in the legs now and the cold had started getting to him through the grease coating.

And then the miracle happened. A killer whale surfaced right in front of him. He could see the white patch next to the eye and then the great fin, even though the moon had not come out. The timing on the part of the whale could not have been better because his strength had given up by then. He embraced his daughter and they went down into the darkness and the deep.

❖ THE TUNNEL ❖

Everyone who knew Greta and Jon—both their friends and those who envied them—had been trying for a long time to find fault with their life and happy marriage but had not succeeded. The reason for this was nothing special, only the human condition.

The two of them were close, perfectly happy together, didn't drink to excess and had never been unfaithful to each other. They had been married for almost forty years now and had early on marked out their own territory. A tacit agreement had come up of its own accord. On the surface Greta was a jovial woman, a highly educated and well respected lawyer, but she also had a heavy undercurrent running through her, and had only to give her husband a certain kind of a look when there was a danger of a disagreement coming on. And then he was only too happy to back down—he considered subordinating his will to hers as an indication of how much and how deeply he loved her. As a result, the house they had in the hills overlooking the best part of town and the summerhouse they had on an expensive lot at the seaside, with the speedboat they would use to inspect the birdlife out on the island they owned, was really her domain, while he was absolute master of the popular Italian restaurant they ran in town. They both looked very young for their age. The psychiatrist told their daughter Isabelle that there are many who fall for a beautiful face without having any idea that a hateful stranger lives behind it. They had never needed a psychiatrist, because they hadn't set out in their youth with masks made of their dreams in search of someone beautiful to hang them on. They had been perfect for each other from the start. Theirs was the good life.

They had four children and nine grandchildren and August 18, 2014, would be their fortieth wedding anniversary. Their children decided that this was a good occasion for a grand family reunion and had therefore coached the keys of the summerhouse from their mother's hands—the idea was to hold a surprise feast for their father.

Jon, of course unaware of his children's plans, had decided to close the restaurant on this special evening, which was a Saturday, and have the whole place decorated with shiny white tablecloths. Only one table was to be set in the middle of the room, with two lit candles, symbolizing himself and his wife. The other unset tables were also to be a symbol of the fact that in their lives there had really been only the two of them.

They often used to call themselves "soulmates" in the company of others, something that their daughter Isabelle had been hearing since she was an infant, something that now made her so irritated that she was on the verge of screaming, as her own marriage was in tatters.

On the morning of August 18, Jon gave his wife a handsome sum of money so she could go buy herself the gift she longed for—he had long since given up on buying her presents only to find out that she would always return them after a lengthy discussion with herself. He then told her that he wanted to invite her to dine at their restaurant that evening, since he had something special in store for her.

This made her laugh, and she stared at him with that special look in her eye that told him he shouldn't push the matter any further. But he did so anyway, saying, "Darling, this is really important to me, and you will realize why when we get there this evening."

"It sounds both corny and ludicrous," was her reply. "I want to spend this special weekend at the summerhouse."

"That sounds even more ludicrous to me," he said, feeling a vague irritation.

"But it's very important to me," she said.

"Why?"

"Well, if you absolutely must know, the children will be there, giving a surprise party in our honor."

"In that case I'll just call the restaurant and say there's been a change of plans. It's no problem," he said, and he picked up the phone and gave the chef instructions to open back up for the public that evening. When he put down the phone he saw that his wife had been looking at him with awe at what he had arranged for her. He had taken great care that she would learn as much as possible from listening to the conversation.

They got into their car, a large SUV of the most expensive kind. There was heavy traffic since the day was extremely beautiful. On the mountain, occasional dark patches momentarily shielded the sun. The sea was tranquil, responding to the clouds by shifting colors from green to gray.

"Strange," Jon said suddenly. "It is as if there's no rule to nature. It's all a coincidence. There's no system for how the clouds pass before the sun."

"That's right," she said. "As a lawyer I've handled many divorce cases, but there have been times when neither myself nor a priest could prevent disaster from happening. Sometimes no amount of reasoning will do. It's as if some of these marriages run their course in little shut rooms where no moral principles apply. I ask you to forgive me for insisting on going to the summerhouse but we're not going there for our own sakes. I want to do all I can to prevent Isabelle's marriage from breaking up."

"That's good," he said. "The condition of things in their home has been worrying me for a while."

She laid a hand on his, which was on the steering wheel, and it took him by surprise, causing the car to sway a little. "But thank you for the dinner you had so carefully planned for the two of us this evening."

"It's okay to skip it," he said. "I've had a good life with you. And perhaps we will be able to prevent the end of our daughter's marriage, but there's always only so much you can do. We're always subject to chance. For example, when lightning strikes an airplane, causing it to crash, or when someone who has been a model driver his whole life loses control of his car and rams it into oncoming traffic at high speed. Such a thing might happen, for example, in the tunnel just ahead or on the road around the fjord.

"Let's drive around the fjord," she suddenly said. "I always find the darkness and the lights in the tunnel so uncomfortable."

"But that will add more than an hour, even close to ninety minutes, to our trip, and we are already late," he said.

His wife was about to say something when he put out a hand. "Don't give me that look," he said with a smile. "You preferred the summerhouse to the restaurant. Now we will take the tunnel."

❖ GIMME SHELTER ❖

THE CAT WAS CLAWING AT THE NEIGHBOR'S DOOR WHEN JIM CAME down the hallway with the bag of groceries.

"Wrong door, kitty kat," Jim said. He put the bags down and rummaged through his pockets for the keys.

The cat was meowing and nuzzling up against the door so much that Jim began to worry that it might cause the old man who lived in the apartment to come out to see what was going on. He picked up the cat and stroked it affectionately, and with the cat in his arms he opened his own apartment for the both of them. He put the bags of groceries on the floor and when he turned around to close the door he saw the old man peering at him from the other side of the hallway. He nodded and the old man did the same.

Ever since the stripper had moved in with Jim he had felt uncomfortable around his neighbors. There was little chance the neighbors would ever find out what she did—the block was full of mostly old folks—but he couldn't help feeling uncomfortable about it anyway.

Jim was a heavyset bald guy in his mid-forties and he could hardly believe his luck. He had gone with a few of his friends to the strip club— it was a kind of mutual hysteria, a shared madness, that had arisen in the taxicab, and before he knew it they were all on their way to Casino Royale, as the club was called. The name came from some old James Bond movie.

It was the kind of strip club you'd find in a movie. A long, dark corridor, a bar, leather sofas where the girls were sitting, a platform where the dancers swung from one pole to the next. Jim was standing at the bar when suddenly she was beside him, a tall thin girl with long black hair and a beak of a nose. She said she was from Romania. "You take great care now," was the first thing she said. "Don't you fall in love with me." Then she gave him a single spank with one swift motion, which caught him off guard.

"What kind of a work you do?" she asked him.

He told her he was a mechanic.

"I like mechanics," she said. "My ex-boyfriend was a mechanic."

She didn't offer him a private dance. Some kind of festival was going on at the strip joint. It was issuing its yearly calendar with pinup pictures of the girls and free drinks and sandwiches were being handed out. When the manager of the place and his cronies realized that Jim and his friends were not on the guest list, a monster of a man with tattooed biceps and the neck of a bull showed them the door. He had a black crew cut and even more tattoos on his huge forearms. The girl, however, whose name was Alexandra, had been impressed by Jim's line of work. This must have been in some way connected with her feelings for her ex-boyfriend. When they were all asked to leave, she took the strip club's card and with one swift motion wrote her cell phone number on it and asked him to call her the following day. He stuck the card in the breast pocket of his white shirt. In the cab his friends were already telling exaggerated versions of their exploits at the strip club and were swearing that the bouncer was queer. Jim felt strangely happy with the card in his breast pocket. The result of the phone call the following day was that the girl had agreed to meet him downtown and the next day she showed up right on time.

The rest was history, a remarkable one to Jim and his family and friends.

"Hush now, boy," Jim said to the cat, which was clawing at his bag in the same manner he had clawed at the old man's door. "It's dinnertime, I know."

He went to the kitchen for a sharp knife and then took the bag of cat food and cut it open on one corner. He put a portion of the food in the cat's bowl but to his surprise the cat only sniffed at it and then went into the living room with a heavy gait, looking like a miniature tiger.

The man found this strange. The cat was getting heavier and heavier as the weeks went by and yet it seemed to have completely lost its appetite.

Alexandra came out of the bathroom wearing a gown. She had tied up her hair in a knot even though Jim liked it best free-flowing. "Any mail?" she asked. The mailbox was out in the hallway.

"Only newspapers, bills, and stuff," Jim said. He knew she was waiting for mail from her home country. Letters came now and then. It didn't bother him. They were mostly from her mother and occasionally from a sister. The only thing he feared was that the mechanic across the ocean would change his mind about her. He felt somehow that this man all those many thousands of miles away was part of her sadness, her discontent.

She sat down at the kitchen table. From the table you could see the door that lead out to the hallway. She was sulking.

"What's the matter, Alexandra?" he asked nervously.

"You promised to buy me a house."

"Well, I married you, didn't I?"

"You did that for selfish reasons," she said.

"Of course I did. Isn't love always selfish?"

"I wouldn't know anything about that," she said. In her reply lay hidden the fact that she had not married him for love but only to be able to stay in the country, and this was a matter that worried Jim greatly.

"I know what you're thinking," she said, and a look of mockery came into her eyes. "But you're wrong, and I've told you so many times. It wasn't because I didn't want to get sent home that I married you. I married you because, I, uh...like you."

"Can't you say you love me?" He had bought her contract from the owner of the strip joint for a considerable sum. She never mentioned it. Neither of them had ever mentioned it.

"You use words like that very freely in your country. And you know I have had many, uh"—and for lack of a better word, she said—"lovers."

"I've been with women too," he said embarrassed. "I've never held that against you."

"So buy me the house you promised me," she said.

The cat was now clawing more insistently at the door. It wanted to go out into the hallway.

"That damn cat," she said. "It somehow gets on my nerves. It's so... so snobbish in some strange way."

Everybody seemed snobbish to her, Jim thought. His brother and his family were snobbish. His sister was snobbish. His friend was snobbish. Even the old man across the hallway was snobbish. Jim rose rather stiffly from the table, where he had been sitting opposite her, and went to tend to the cat. It slipped out as soon as he opened the door.

He turned around. "Okay," he said. "I'll buy you the house. I always keep my promises. Today is Friday. Tomorrow and Sunday we'll go house-hunting."

The Saturday paper carried a supplement with real estate ads. He went to get it from the mailbox as soon as he woke up on Saturday morning. The cat had not come home the previous evening but he was not worried about it yet.

They had their morning coffee and toast while leafing through the real estate ads and pointed out houses to each other that they liked. "I want a house with a large yard...for the children," she said, and when he became flushed with happiness and tried to hide it, she gave him a quick slap on the forearm, in the same way that she'd slapped him on the butt on the evening they first met each other.

As usual it took her far longer to get dressed, so he went out and began looking for the cat. By now the length of the animal's absence had begun to worry him. "Kitty cat," he said, "where are you?"

But out in the hallway there was only the silence of a Saturday morning. He went down the stairs and out into the cool February morning. It had rained during the night and his Jeep Grand Cherokee was wet. He walked back and forth on the pavement in front of the house calling for the cat. Behind him on the hill, a bit higher than the apartment complex, cars thundered by on the road. Suddenly the man became afraid that the cat might have been hit by a car. From his kitchen window he had sometimes seen the cat cross the road, taking great risks as it did so. A few cats had been killed on that road. He remembered witnessing one particular cat being run over. The cat, its intestines crushed, had done a crazy dance on the road and jumped incredibly high into the air. Jim walked up the wet, grassy hill to the parking lot that lead to the road and looked around. There wasn't a dead cat to be seen. After a moment he made his way down the slope again. At about the same time that his wife appeared in the entrance of the apartment complex, a window opened on the third floor. It was the old man who lived on the other side of the hallway. "Are you looking for your cat?" he called down.

"Yeah," Jim said, staring at the old man. "Have you seen him?"

"He's with me," the old man said.

"What's he saying?" Alexandra asked. She was standing on the sidewalk now.

"He says he's got our cat."

Alexandra looked up toward the old man in the window and he looked down at the couple with a strange gleeful expression that seemed to indicate that the cat was now his. This irritated Jim. "Wait a minute," Jim said to Alexandra while fumbling through his pockets for the keys to the house. The house keys and the car keys were fastened to the same key chain.

She held out a hand. "Let me start the car," she said. "I'm cold."

He opened the front door and reluctantly handed her the keys. She liked to drive but he didn't like her to. He loved his car and she was a reckless driver. "I'm coming up," he called to the old man just as his kitchen window was closing.

The door to the old man's apartment was ajar when Jim arrived on the third floor. He opened it further and by doing so saw into the parlor. The cat was sitting on the sofa surrounded by pillows. It was watching TV. The old man came into view. He had lost his wife two years earlier and his children seldom visited him. The cat paid Jim no attention and kept on watching the television. Next to the sofa, under the window, which looked out in the opposite direction from the parking lot and the road, were two bowls placed side by side on an old newspaper.

"Come here, boy," Jim called softly, but the cat continued to watch the morning program.

"He likes watching television," the old man said, "but he likes even more the food I give him." The old man pointed to the bowls under the window. "Fresh milk is what I give him, and shrimp."

111

"I give him cat food," Jim replied a bit feebly.

"He likes the shrimp boiled," the old man said. "But not too much. Just dropped quickly into boiling water. That's the way to do it. He adores them like that."

"Come on, He-Man. Come on, boy," Jim said.

"I call him Hustler," the old man said.

"Hustler?" Jim asked, looking at the old man.

"Yes. He's so soft when you pet him. He reminds me of...well, you know," the old man said with a glint in his eyes, "the magazine."

"The magazine," Jim repeated. "Yes, I know which magazine you're referring to." He suddenly heard his wife honk the horn of the jeep impatiently. The gleam in the old man's eyes intensified and Jim looked away uncomfortably. There was a mild smell of urine in the apartment and it didn't come from the cat. Jim looked at the old man again. He was bald and had brown blotches on his face and a small, soft stomach.

Alexandra kept on honking the horn.

"You better go," the old man said. "Your wife is calling you." His mouth was hanging open now and his expression was almost lustful, as far as Jim could tell. What the hell is going on? Jim thought. He felt desperate. Had the old bastard been to the strip club? "Well, thanks for taking care of the cat," he said. "I'll pick it up in a couple hours or so."

"That'll be fine," the old man said, seeming normal. "You want me to switch to another channel, Hustler, old boy," was the last thing Jim heard the old man say as he left the apartment and closed the door on the two of them.

Jim tiptoed down the stairs, feeling bad about leaving the animal with a stranger. He had a few stairs yet to go when Alexandra started honking the horn again. She stopped when he came out the door. Jim went up to the driver's-side window and she slid it down.

"Please let me drive, honey," she said before he could open his mouth.

"I'd rather drive," he said. "We'll make it quicker to all the houses I've picked out if I drive."

"Let me drive to the first house," she said. "You can direct me. And then you can take over."

He had picked out five houses in the neighborhood where he'd been born and raised. The first one was so run-down they didn't even have to get out of the car. The second and the third didn't have the yard they were hoping for, but the fourth one was a dream. And they were lucky—there was an open house that day. A couple was coming out of the house. After Jim and Alexandra walked through the house, Jim had practically made up his mind. When the owner needed to take a brief call on his cell phone, Jim told Alexandra not to look so obviously happy with the whole thing since her expression would only result in keeping the price high. She began to pout immediately. "This way we'll get a better deal," he whispered. "Houses are difficult to sell these days, especially the more expensive ones with two floors and a garage, like this one."

When they had inspected the whole thing, they decided not to inspect the fifth house on the list, although Alexandra insisted they go and take a quick look at it just to be on the safe side. They had practically made up their minds. Once they had driven slowly past the fifth house and decided they had already found their future home, Jim looked worriedly at his watch. It was a few minutes past five.

"Are you worried about something, darling?" Alexandra said. "Don't be. I'm so happy. When we get home I will cook you a great dinner. And then, you know"—she nudged closer to him—"then we can go to bed."

He nodded, looking happy but more absentminded than he ought to be. He was worried about the cat.

"Are you worried about something?" she asked again.

"No," he replied.

They stopped at the supermarket on the way home. He knew it would take her quite a while to do her shopping so he called up an old school friend who was a lawyer and told him about the house he wanted to buy. He directed him to the ad in the paper and asked him to make an offer on his behalf. When he'd done this he called the same real estate agent who was advertising the house and put his apartment up for sale. The real estate agent said he expected the apartment to sell easily, since it was situated in a popular part of town and apartments were much easier to sell these days. They agreed that the agent would show up the following day and inspect the apartment and take a few photographs. Everything was settled by the time Alexandra returned with her grocery bags. Jim drove them home and parked the car in front of their complex, then opened the building's door for his wife and carried the bags up the stairs. The old man was waiting in the hallway when they came up to the third floor.

"Good evening, ma'am," he said politely to Alexandra, but Jim thought the tone of his voice sounded strange.

Jim put the grocery bags down and handed the keys to Alexandra so she could open the door of their apartment, and then he turned towards the old man's apartment to get the cat.

"There's no need to hurry," the old man said. "He's having such a fine time with me, the old boy."

The old man was blocking his way. "Well," Jim said, "I'm grateful to you for being so kind to him, but I would like to take him home now, if you don't mind."

"Of course," the old man said, stepping out of the doorway so that Jim could go inside. The TV was off but the cat was still on the sofa surrounded by pillows. How well Jim knew the familiar touch when he lifted him up by the belly. The cat was heavy and limp but then suddenly came to life and let out a great meow, and kept on hanging on to the sofa by his claws. It took a bit of struggle to free him from the sofa and Jim found it embarrassing. He had had the cat for a long time, twelve years to be exact, and it hurt him that the animal was such an opportunist.

"He's welcome to stay," the old man said.

"No, thanks," Jim said a bit curtly. "Come on, He-Man." At last he freed the cat from the sofa.

"I'll be seeing you, Hustler," the old man said to the cat as they were leaving.

"His name is He-Man," Jim said.

"Okay, so be it," the old man said, and then he closed the door.

The dinner and the evening followed without incident. The following day was Sunday and Jim kept a careful watch over He-Man to make sure the cat wouldn't be tempted to slip over to the old man. But the cat was at the door all day long, clawing and meowing and trying to get out. A bit later in the day, Jim's friend the lawyer called back and said the owner of the house was willing to make a deal, but he wanted five-thousand more than Jim had offered.

"What would you do in my place?" Jim asked.

"Tell him no. The town is close to bursting with unsold houses. I would have told him no myself but I thought it would be better to get your consent."

"Okay, you got my consent."

The lawyer called back five minutes later. Jim's and Alexandra's offer had been accepted.

On Monday when they left for work, Jim let the cat out with some misgivings. When work was over he went to pick up his wife. She worked at a cleaners to supplement their income. From Jim's point of view it wasn't a permanent job. He hoped that they would soon have a child.

"Well, how are you?" His wife gave him a quick kiss on the cheek once she got into the car.

"I'm fine. I got a call from the guy selling the apartment for us. He said that at least four interested parties had phoned, and two are coming over this evening to take a look. We can move into the house later this week or next weekend. I've already spoken to my brothers—they're going to help and John has called a guy with a truck who is giving us a good deal. So a week from now, you'll be living in your own house!"

She let out a cry of joy.

When they got home the cat was nowhere to be found.

"You should lock him up if it means so much to you," Alexandra said.

Jim sighed and went across the hallway and knocked politely on the old man's door. He saw the cat on the sofa as the door opened, even before he saw the face of the old man.

"He's been having such a good time with me," the old man said. "I cooked him some cod today—new cod, freshly caught—and he simply loved it."

Jim looked at the cat but the cat didn't look at him.

"He's following this soap opera," the old man said, laughing. The old man had a rather pleasant laugh and Jim suddenly decided to accept things as they were and make use of him. They would be busy the whole week selling the apartment and then moving and it made sense to let the old geezer take care of the cat. They would move this coming weekend and the old man would be out of their lives anyway.

The first couple who came to inspect the apartment that evening bought it.

They moved the following weekend so He-Man spent all that week with the old man. After Jim's brothers had spent all of Saturday and the better part of Sunday moving their belongings to the other side of town, Jim's last job before leaving the apartment was to go pick up his cat. The house they were moving into was so big that the old cat would have an entire room all to himself. The cat made a scene and hung onto the sofa like it had done when Jim went to pick it up the first time.

Jim felt himself quietly cursing under his breath, yet he managed to thank the old man for taking care of the cat during this busy week. "I don't know how we would have managed without your help," he said, and he hoped the old man would not detect the falseness in his voice.

If the old man did, he didn't seem to care. "I'll be seeing you," he said to the cat.

Well, I rather doubt that, Jim thought. He let himself into his empty apartment and walked around it one last time. The place looked forlorn when empty and for a brief moment he found it strange that he had ever lived there. The cat was struggling with him and wanted to be let loose. "Be quiet, boy. Take it easy," Jim said.

Jim drove across town and let the cat inspect his own room for the first time. His food bowl was full of cereal and his water bowl full of clean, fresh water. The cat inspected all this and then looked at Jim. For the first time since the animal was a kitten, Jim had the strange feeling that after twelve years they didn't know each other at all.

He closed the door on the cat. He found the feeling of alienation from the animal disturbing.

He had ordered ten pizzas for the gang that had helped him move. He had made a point not to buy any beer since he didn't want a drunken spree to be the first event in his new home. Yet the crew was laughing and joking so much that they all seemed more or less intoxicated.

Alexandra was putting things in their place in the house when Jim came home from work the following day. Two of her friends, both foreign and former dancers, were helping out. It was an overwhelming assembly of female beauty, and Jim left them to check out the cat, which seemed ill at ease. He let it out to explore the yard and it looked around with a look of satisfaction.

Jim opened up the garage. He was handy with his large assortment of tools and he looked forward to arranging them there. Now, for the first time in his life, he had a large garage, so large that it was easy for him to take on extra work at home. He closed the garage door and locked it. When he looked around for the cat, it was gone.

He walked around the house looking for it. Quiet desperation was rising within him. The cat was nowhere to be seen. He went out again and inspected the yard carefully. Then he walked around the neighborhood and called out the animal's name, to no avail. The cat was gone. Jim thought of the old man. No, it wasn't possible! That was too far away and the cat wouldn't be able to find its way across town. Most likely he was offended by the move and, to rebel, had hid. He had showed his displeasure that way before.

Dusk began to settle on the town. At nightfall the cat still hadn't returned. Not knowing what had happened to the animal, Jim went to bed in the new house for the first time.

The following day after work he drove straight to the old man's. He had to ring the doorbell now for the first time to be let into his former building. "Who is it?" a voice said.

"It's Jim," Jim replied, "your former neighbor. I've lost my cat." He was about to begin to explain through the intercom how ridiculous his situation was but the old man didn't wait to listen—the screaming buzzer when he opened the door blotted out Jim's voice. The old man was standing out in the hallway when Jim came up the stairs.

"He's here," the old man said.

The cat was sitting in the sofa as before. The animal's air of satisfaction filled Jim with anger.

"Can't you let me have him?" the old man asked. "You see, the thing is, I'm all alone. You know that my wife died and I miss her greatly. The animal likes me and I love to feed him all the goodies my wife used to eat. By some strange coincidence they like the same things."

"Lots of people like shrimp," Jim replied rather abruptly as he picked up the cat.

"Can't you let him live with me?" the old man implored.

"I'm sorry," Jim said. "It's all pretty ridiculous from my point of view."

They stood facing each other for a moment.

When the old man realized Jim's refusal was final, he regarded Jim with great hostility and said, "There's something I would like to show you."

"What is it?" Jim asked once he had managed to pull the cat loose from the sofa.

Then the old man seemed to think better of it. "Oh, nothing," the old man said.

Jim left. For the next few days he kept a close eye on the cat and wouldn't let him out of his room.

On Thursday a brown envelope came for Jim in the mail. Alexandra was busy cleaning the house and had left all the windows open. The following day, Friday, would be the housewarming party, and Jim's brothers and Alexandra's friends would be coming over to celebrate. It was customary to hold a party for those who had helped to move and clean the house.

Jim sat down and opened the mail. The handwriting on the brown envelope seemed familiar, and suddenly he realized where he had seen it before. He had been the head of the committee that saw to it that the apartment building's common areas were kept clean, and the contract for the cleaning woman had to be signed by each of the tenants. The scrawl on the envelope was the old man's. If the old man wanted the identity of the person who'd mailed the envelope to remain secret, he had done a poor job of it.

It was an old porn magazine. Not a major one like *Hustler*, just a small, local one called *Pink and Blue*. It was said to show girls who lived in town and also models who came in to work on special assignment. When he leafed through it he recognized Alexandra immediately, although the two men sharing her were strangers to him. He looked at the photos; they were spread over four pages. He closed the magazine and put it away in a cupboard he could close with a key.

He felt in some strange, absent frame of mind for the rest of the evening. He felt as if nothing out of the ordinary had happened. When they had eaten he went to check on the cat, but Alexandra had also left open the window of the room where the cat lived and the cat was gone. Jim realized that it must have already gone far. It was not yet dark. There was still hope that he might be able to catch the cat before it got to the old man.

He drove towards the other side of town. The big interstate highway that bisected the town had a bridge in the middle of it, and when Jim approached the highway he saw He-Man halfway across the bridge, heading in the old man's direction. Jim decided not to go any farther. The cat was lost to him anyway and sooner or later he would have to face the old man, and right on the heels of receiving the magazine in the mail he couldn't picture himself doing that.

He drove home. The following day at work he felt like a zombie. Things happened around him and yet they were somehow not happening at all. It was a situation that was hard to describe, or so it seemed to him.

The housewarming party was in the evening. He drank more than usual and gradually felt, thanks to the beer and wine, that his old self was returning. He conversed amiably with his brothers and yet he couldn't quite stop thinking about the magazine. The girls were all getting drunk. And suddenly one of Jim's brothers shouted in jest, "You should install a pole in the living room so they can dance right here! Hell, there isn't a soul in town who hasn't seen up your wife's crotch anyway!"

"Now you shut your filthy mouth," Jim's other brother said.

"What am I being scolded for?" the first one said. "Jim, you know I didn't mean to offend you. It's just me and my big mouth. It's just the way I am. I can't help it. You all know that."

Jim nodded. Life was somehow taking him by such surprise that he didn't have time to react to anything.

A moment later he found himself in the garage, where he had already sorted out his tools. He turned on the light and picked up one of the most effective ones, an axe.

He took a big swig from the vodka bottle he had taken along for comfort. Then he started the long walk across town with the bottle in hand, taking a swig now and then. He would be at his destination before dawn. It didn't occur to him to drive. From his point of view he didn't have anything illegal in mind.

A cold wind was howling when he got to the bridge. Walking across it and seeing the highway empty for the first time, he knew at once how the world must look to a cat—or, for that matter, to its larger relative, the tiger.

❖ THE REVELATION ❖

In the house across the street lived the most beautiful girl I'd ever seen. She was way out of my league. She didn't mingle with people as ugly as me. She was two years older. I adored her. And all she ever did if I tried to talk to her was make faces at me.

When the Rolling Stones became popular, however, my ugliness, as opposed to being a handicap, became something to treasure. If only I had a voice to match my face I would've become the singer, rather than the roadie, of the group Linda's brothers were forming in the summer of '65.

Her name was Linda.

I won't try to describe her. I'm not a writer so I can't. I can only say that if she had ever appeared in Playboy she would've put all the other centerfolds to shame. She would definitely have been Playmate of the Year.

As for her brothers, each one was unique in his own special way, just as each bad tooth differs from the next one. Only Little Joe was so beautiful that he could be called the good tooth.

I told you right from the start that I wasn't a writer. A real writer would begin his story at the beginning, and my beginning is this: Once upon a time, when both Linda and I were children, we had an exhibition of all our toys. Each of us put our toys up for the other to admire in the living room windows of our facing apartments.

Perhaps because I was an only child—she had four brothers—I was the winner. I had far more toys to put in my windowsill, and suddenly her curtains were drawn. I must have been no more than ten years old.

Well, anyhow. When I was seventeen I got my driver's license, which stood me in good stead with the group, since they needed a roadie. The group, with good reason was simply called the Winos, and they were getting more and more bookings all the time.

The night before this story really starts, we'd come home from a gig in the countryside in our sad, old, rickety van and I had been too tired to unload the gear, which was my job. So as soon as I got up the following morning, I wandered across the street to put the instruments into the garage.

When I entered the garage I noticed that the old man was lying there on a mattress, which meant that he had been banned from sleeping inside the house. Which meant he was on a bender.

When the sunlight fell into the garage through the open door, he raised his head in reply and then hauled himself to his feet. He was a sight to behold, a Keith Richards lookalike. I'm willing to bet his body was able to withstand at least as much drugs and alcohol.

He staggered over to the workbench where he kept all his tools. There stood a bottle of Southern Comfort, and he took an enormous swig from it. I could see the hard liquor going down his gullet by the steady movement of his Adam's apple. Then he beckoned me with an index finger to come over. I did as instructed, though a bit warily— you could never be sure what was coming from his direction once the liquor took hold.

As soon as I was within his grasp he grabbed me by the collar and belched right into my face. Then he slung me up against the wall underneath a calendar with a gorgeous pinup girl on it and demanded I take a swig from the bottle. I did as I was told and the liquor burned all the way down my throat.

Then he shook his head for a long time with a look of utter disapproval. He took hold of my long hair and shook his head a while more. When he was finally able to get out a word he said sorrowfully, "George…George, I always figured you for a real man." His face was so woebegone it was almost as if he'd just lost some close relative. "George, I always thought you'd grow up to be a fine young man, and to tell you the truth I had high hopes for you. I wanted you to inherit my business, George, and I'm now taking about things not meant to be brought out into the open at this point in time." He took a pause now to take another swig. "I wanted you to inherit more than my business. I wanted you to marry my daughter and that's the truth. But then you grew long hair, like my four good-for-nothin' sons, and, George"—he sadly shook his head—"I just don't know anymore what to think. And now Linda is running around with a no-good layabout....I'm losin' control, George. I'll soon be an old man. The world is spinnin' around so fast I cant get through to anyone any more. " And he continued shaking his head, overcome by it all.

Needless to say, I would've gotten a crew cut right then and there if I had known it would do me any good where Linda was concerned.

The fact is that she'd taken up with a guy all the girls were dying to go out with. It was beyond human comprehension what all of them saw in this nitwit. I once sat next to him in a booth at a hamburger joint downtown and heard him sweet-talk some girl and, my God, like I said before, I'm not claiming to be a poet or anything, but the clichés, you'd never heard anything like it. As for an example this: "It's like the starry heavens have stepped down and settled in your eyes," was one of the things he uttered. I thought the girl would break out laughing and mock him like he deserved, but when I glanced quickly around I saw that her face had turned beet red and her eyes were moist.

I hadn't yet come to grips with how a piece of pure gold like Linda could have bought such crap. But obviously she had. Even so, my love for her hadn't diminished one bit. It must be some misunderstanding, her going out with this guy, and I was sure she had to wise up some time.

Her father's truck stood outside in the street. He ran a gardening business. It was a bold move on his part since he wasn't a gardener at all. A whole suburb was being created around Reykjavík at the time and Linda's old man had a few employees, and then he had recently bought a machine from abroad, a grass-cutting tool, a wonderful gadget with shiny knives of steel at the bottom like the jaws of a great white.

The Winos worked for the gardening business all week and then there were gigs on the weekends. "George," the old man said. "You seem to be doin' a good job of holdin' the Winos together, keeping the lid on what they call 'musical differences,' whatever those are, and gettin' them to gigs on time. I want you to help us in the gardening too! Then you can wake them up in the mornings and get them goin'. The season is short and I need to make as much money as I can this summer."

I gladly accepted his offer. It gave me a chance to be closer to Linda.

And so it happened that I became a foreman as well as a roadie. On the weekends we played the Yardbirds, the Kinks, the Searchers, the Swinging Blue Jeans, not to mention the Beatles and the Stones. There were always a lot of girls who were hot for the band, but I was still a virgin, ugly-looking fuckface that I was. It really got to me. My only comfort was that I'd read in some magazine that no man was so grotesquely ugly that there wasn't somewhere a woman that found him attractive. The thing was to find that woman.

Right then that morning my task was to wake the boys and gather the tools onto the truck and rush off to work. I accidentally opened the door to Linda's room and my heart skipped when I saw her sleeping there with her boyfriend. I closed the door in a hurry and turned my attention to the boys. They got out of bed grumbling, and asked me if I had a screw loose, waking them at this hour, and why the hell did I look so downcast.

The truck was a green 1955 Chevrolet and had seen better days. The old man had recently gotten the job to fix the grounds of a new mansion that some doctor had built in one of the new suburbs. A lot of dirt had to be driven there to make the lawn flat, and that was our task for the following two days. Two of the brothers, Ben, the drummer—who was said to be the hardest-hitting drummer in the northern hemisphere—and Adam, who played bass, were then driven to some grassy area by the old man in his Land Rover, with the grass-cutting machine on a trailer hitched to the back.

It was driven by a gasoline motor. You started it up and then held on to the handlebars and followed the vibrating contraption while it cut the grass into long swaths. The idea was to snake through the grass, turning it into boxlike bits of turf ready to be shoveled on the bed of the Chevy truck.

By the time the weekend rolled around there was a lawn around the mansion, and we had even planted some Christmas trees. After the old man got paid by the doctor and his wife, he, Hoss and Hop Sing left. This happened on a Friday. They returned in the most amazingly beautiful sedan I'd ever seen in my life, a 1959 Chrysler. The old man was drunk, of course—both from Southern Comfort and joy—and so proud of the car that he decided he would follow The Winos to their next gig, which would be a new experience for his sons. In addition to being the roadie, I was the group's agent, and thus I booked the gigs. This time we were headed about thirty miles out of Reykjavík.

I drove the Chrysler. Linda and her boyfriend were necking in the backseat. The boys followed in the van with the gear. The Chrysler was a great car to drive and I kept a steady eye on the boys in the van. But my real reason for driving it was to take a peak at Linda now and then in the mirror. The car was a convertible and her blond hair streamed out behind her in the wind like an aurora—I can't describe it any better.

I saw the youngest brother, Johannes, climb onto the roof of the van. His brothers had renamed him Little Joe because he looked like the youngest brother in the TV series *Bonanza*. In turn I had nicknamed the rest of the brothers Ben, Adam, Hoss and Hop Sing, the last one after the farm's Chinese cook. *Bonanza* was the most popular program on the American forces TV channel that summer. We never missed *Bonanza*.

Ever since he was born, Little Joe had to prove himself constantly. He had been jumping off garages and crawling through barbed-wire fences as long as I could remember. His hands were always scratched. He had an old, deep scar going all the way from the temple down to the chin. There was always a hint of fear in his eyes. I guess his brothers gave him his nickname to torment him, since his handsome face set him so much apart from the rest of them. But Linda took care of him. He was her protégé.

When we arrived at the dance, most of the country people were already drunk on local moonshine. With the help of Linda's boyfriend, I set up the drums and the amplifier. He must have known how I felt about her because, like an idiot, he constantly had a stupid grin on his face. The Winos started playing at ten o'clock and carried on till one in the morning. Though they'd recorded two or three singles that had been pretty popular, they'd never achieved the same ferocious atmosphere in the studio as they did at dances. (I still have these records. On one of them it says, "Thanks to George for bringing beer while recording.") The place was packed. Although most were young, there were also the odd oldie turned up, farmers from the surrounding area. I saw the old man talking to one of them. They were already thick as thieves. The old man had a slack, dazed expression from the liquor. The other fellow was eyeing him with what seemed to me to be a look of disdain. I made my way over to them through the crowd. I ran into Linda, who was dancing with some farmhand, and I asked her if she shouldn't keep an eye on her old man, but she replied sharply, "What good would that do? Haven't you seen my mother?" I got her point. At little more than forty years of age, Linda's mother looked older than my grandmother.

When I got over to the old man, he put his arm around my shoulders and introduced me to the sly-looking farmer in the manner that drunks do. He said that I was his most trusted employee and his future son-in-law, and so on and so forth, and then he ordered me to drive him and the farmer to look at some piece of land the farmer wanted the old man to buy. The land was filled with gravel, which was used for roads and as a base for foundations. The way the farmer figured, for a man in the turf-laying business it could come in handy to own a gravel pit. On our way there, the farmer pointed out with great pride a new barn he had built at some tremendous cost. The old man was either too drunk or too lazy to be bothered getting out of the car. He sat in the Chrysler taking swigs from his Southern Comfort. I went and had a look at the quarry. It was nothing but an enormous dark pit with steep walls and a narrow, dangerous-looking road leading down to it. If you dug any further from the side there was a chance that the whole mountain would come tumbling down.

It was obvious the farmer thought he had found a sucker he could easily hustle. One look at the old man confirmed my suspicion that he was too drunk to be reasoned with. Although I was doing the driving, he insisted that I join them in the drinking. I did as I was told, taking small sips and holding onto the bottle, mostly to stop him from getting any drunker.

The dance was in full swing when we returned and I had gained some unexpected courage. Sitting on the floor, I fondly stroked the silken thigh of some girl who was sitting on the table above. She sent me an encouraging smile. She didn't seem to mind my ugly face but when I tried to take advantage of the situation and rose to ask her to dance, I found myself face to face with a hostile-looking boyfriend. I got really drunk that night, which rarely happened. The only thing I remember is a seething darkness, with sometimes faces appearing through it, and snatches of this or that song.

I woke up in a gray, wet dawn, alone and groggy, rain falling on my face, while a friendly sheep not far away was munching on some straw.

I vaguely recalled telling the Winos to go to hell and that they could goddamn very well pack up their gear for themselves and look after their old man.

I had also claimed that they "would be nothing without me," which sounded more than a little ludicrous in my hung-over state. The van was gone, the Chrysler was gone, and I had to hitchhike back to town. Deep in my mind I knew what was behind it all—it was my love for Linda.

I let Sunday pass before I wandered across the street in the evening to put things right. I fully expected to get fired, but instead they were slapping my back like some goddamn war hero. "We didn't think you were such a rebel, Georgie boy!" Later on my rebellious spirit would surprise even their sister.

The summer wore on. We played an untold number of gigs and fixed more gardens. While climbing the stairs in the house across the street one Sunday morning, I heard strange noises. When I came to the hallway where you went into the family apartment through three doors I noticed that the door to Linda's bedroom stood half open. I could see her on top of her boyfriend, fucking him. Nothing of their lovemaking passed me by. I saw her lovely blond hair and her curving back. Her boyfriend's eyes and mine met. He was resting his head on a pillow. He neither gestured for me to go away nor did he make Linda aware of the fact that there was somebody watching. He only smiled at me with his hands folded beneath his head.

I slipped into the kitchen very suddenly feeling thirsty. I filled a glass with cold water and took a drink and felt a little better. Then I went to wake up Linda's father by gently grabbing his foot. He raised his head from his pillow and gave me a grumpy nod. His wife was still asleep. A freckled shoulder could be seen through her thin, red, almost transparent hair, which somehow gave the idea of a much younger woman, until you saw her face. I walked to the kitchen. The door to Linda's room had thank goodness been shut when I came out again. Then I went up to the loft where the brothers were sleeping two to a room. I woke them and told them it was a workday. Then I hurried off to go and wake Joe. He was sleeping in the garage on his father's filthy old mattress. It was the only place he could get any peace and quiet. I told him that even though it was Sunday, we had work to do. Autumn was on its way and we were well behind on some projects, one of them being the first opportunity to profit from the newly acquired gravel pit, since someone needed a foundation filled. I knew there was no gravel there to speak of but ever since the old man bought the land he'd refused to face up to the truth.

We drove out into the country on the truck and the Chrysler. An old, broken-down excavator had been a part of the deal and Little Joe was sent to get it. It took him some time—we could see Joe and the farmer gesticulating, as if the farmer was trying to go back on his word, but finally Joe climbed aboard and started up the monstrosity, which let out a gush of pitch black exhaust, then moved towards us. You could hear a clanking, as it came nearer. Our tired, sad, old truck drove behind it down into the pit, the gearbox howling. Little Joe started the digging, but there was no gravel, nothing but solid rock, which gave off blue smoke and a strange, strong smell as the iron claws scraped it.

Suddenly a neighbor appeared at the barbed-wire fence redder than red and launched a string of abuse, saying the only gravel remaining was on his property and it would be as well for us if we didn't start digging away from under his fence, and if we did he would call the authorities. The old man gave him the evil eye for a moment, and then he just spat in his direction.

The old man then began screaming at Joe from the brink of the pit.

Joe shut the machine down so he could hear his father. "You damn fool!" yelled the old man. "Dig closer to where I'm standing!"

Little Joe did as he was told but all of a sudden the whole side of the pit caved in and buried him. Most of it was the neighbor's land, and the barbed-wire fence dangled in midair like some bridge over a canyon you see in a movie that takes place in South America or some place far away.

The old man gave a yell and jumped down into the ravine and went right for the shovel that was kept under the house of the truck. The brothers floored the Chrysler in direction of the farm for other equipment to dig with.

The neighbor sauntered off towards his house as if nothing had happened. He did not look back and did not return. I started digging like crazy with my bare hands but it was obvious even to me that we would never get to Joe in time.

We didn't find him until the sun was going down. Then the police had arrived and an ambulance and a crowd of onlookers. Suddenly the sand fell away from his face. It was like finding a marble statue that has been buried for two-thousand years in an ancient town of some long-ago civilization under which a volcano stood that exploded.

With Joe's death it was all over. So really I've now told you what happened the summer of '65. After the death of his youngest son, the old man, who'd never been very stable, went insane. Of course it wasn't called insanity at the time, but what else can you call it? He lost interest in everything. He hit the bottle once and for all. And the Winos couldn't earn enough income by themselves to keep the family going. Me, I quit as roadie and agent. I was disgusted with the brothers because of how they treated Joe. The bailiff soon repossessed the Chrysler and the truck. There was nothing else worth anything to meet the debts after the old man swallowed a massive quantity of sleeping pills and downed a whole bottle of Southern Comfort, thereby committing suicide. He was found dead on his dirty mattress one morning.

The claim against him was from the farmer who had sold him the gravel pit.

Was there ever a more shameless man? The landlord, out of the goodness of his heart, promised the family that they could stay in the flat until the end of the year, but then they would have to come up with some of the rent. And there were worse things to come. Legal action was taken by the doctor, the one who needed all the soil in the spring. He maintained we had done a sloppy job on his yard and not up to professional standards and took the matter to court. A pond was forming in the middle of his lawn in the autumn rain.

One evening that winter, Linda came home completely drunk. It was a chilly night, filled with stars and a great stillness. She stood in front of the house mad with rage. I listened in awe. There was an awful silence in the street. I had the feeling that every single soul in the neighborhood was listening as she dressed her brothers and her boyfriend down for being yellow-bellied weaklings for not doing anything about the unjust way the family had been treated and her brother killed. The Winos had broken up by then. Only Ben, the drummer, was good enough to get a job in some group that played regularly at the army base.

The deep frost and the stillness continued. The next evening I took a trip out of town. I had some sawdust in a sack I'd gotten from the furniture factory. I bought a small bottle of turpentine and stole a candle stub from my grandmother. It took me two rides to hitchhike out to the farm. The sky was velvet, the great mountain across the bay black. There was some light coming from the windows of the farmhouse. A long detour got me to the barn, which was unlocked. A breeze was blowing in from the sea.

I got to the barn without the dog barking. My smell was blown in, towards the land.

I made a pile of the sawdust on a bale of hay and stuck the candle right down on top the pile. Then I poured some of the turpentine on it and lit the candle. By the time the flame reached the saw, I would be long gone. The flame burned so prettily in the darkness. I slipped away. As I walked back to town, the intense cold surrounded me. The sky was clear and the Big Dipper bright in the frozen depths. A large moon had come out. When I was about five miles away I could see the fire. When I had walked two more miles I heard the fire trucks. Then they shot past me.

The whole thing was on the front page of all the papers the next day.

The farmer had been uninsured. The total cost of his loss was bound to put him out of business. It wasn't known who had set the fire. The police paid a visit to the family across the street but none of the brothers was called in for questioning.

I somehow felt that although I was merely seventeen, my youth had now come to an end. I was contemplating this, sitting by the window, sadly aware of the fact that I still wasn't fully a man, and at the same time mourning the loss of my childhood where I had sat by the same window showing off my toys to Linda while she showed me all that she had for me to see that was most precious to her.

I was looking at the window reflecting my ugly face when the curtains were suddenly drawn and there she stood before me in all her glory. She was naked, a revelation, a foreboding of the fact that occasionally our dreams become reality.

THE MAN WHO WANTED
❖ TO BE VINCENT ❖

H<small>E CAME UPON AN ACCIDENT AND STOPPED HIS VAN. T</small>HE <small>POLICE</small> had blocked the road. At first Viktor thought a truck had dropped a load of scrap metal but walking closer he saw that that was not the case. He saw the head of a man protruding from beneath the pile of junk. The head was resting on the road. What had seemed to him a pile of iron was in fact a jeep turned upside down from a collision with a truck. A police officer came toward him and motioned for him to go away. "When can I expect to cross the bridge?" Viktor asked, unable to keep his eyes off the man's head.

"It's not likely to be anytime soon. We're waiting for a crane, and tools to cut the man loose. People are advised to take the detour through the woods." Cars had already begun to gather in a line behind Viktor's van. Viktor pulled onto the detour. He rolled down the front window—as a result of seeing the man's head, he was feeling sick. Without being able to control his thoughts, he began to place the head within the frame of a painting. He heard the wail of a siren and an ambulance shot past. The man must be long dead by now, he thought. This would have been a perfect motif for Francis Bacon, the master of contorted faces.

He took the detour through the woods then drove east over the moor. Viktor was a painter. He had been on his way to Mount Hekla to paint the volcano. He was holding an exhibition within a month. He intended to establish himself once and for all. His art had been ignored and it felt like being buried alive. He had never gotten the recognition he deserved.

"It's the asshole story of the human race," an American painter had told him as they drank together one night many years earlier in the American's hotel room in Berlin. As he remembered those words he tried not to let his bitterness get the better of him.

But now all of a sudden an image arose in his mind, a vision of a critic walking into the gallery where the exhibition was to take place. The critic stood on the gleaming parquet floor. Viktor only needed to look into the critic's eyes to know that his review would be devastating. He could see the headline: "VIKTOR PETERSEN MUST DO A DOUBLE SOMERSAULT WHERE HIS ART IS CONCERNED IF HE INTENDS TO BE SOMETHING OTHER THAN A THIRD-RATE VAN GOGH."

"These idiots think that the so-called new painting—or climbing a mountain, setting a table and eating a chicken—they think that's art," Viktor said out loud to himself. Then they have themselves photographed and name the picture "A Chicken Feast on a Mountaintop," he thought. What would Ensor have thought of such a thing? Or Van Gogh?

No, the greatest painters were the classical ones and it was to that source Icelandic art must go to strengthen and refresh itself.

Vincent. Never, ever would Viktor climb out from under his influence. He had once gone to Amsterdam on a pilgrimage to the museum. While walking through the galleries, he felt himself go weak in the knees. He was then in his second year at the art school and the only thing that drove him crazy was not being Vincent van Gogh. He felt like all other paintings were somehow wrong. He couldn't talk about anything other than Vincent's work. After a while he was cruelly teased because of this mania. He was called Viktor Van Gogh. After his first exhibition, "Oh, him, the guy who imitates Van Gogh" had somehow stuck to him.

"I thought I had entered the wrong gallery," one critic wrote in a review of his second exhibition. "I thought Van Gogh was in town. But then I came to and remembered he passed away in 1890."

"Oh, is that so?" Viktor had said to himself when he read the review. "So my paintings are good enough to be taken for the work of the master!" One night when he had been out on a bender with a few other painters, he constantly repeated the critic's confusion but then decided to keep it to himself because he could not bear their laughter. But deep within himself he knew that his paintings were another man's vision, another man's torment.

He stopped his van before the road wound down the mountainside. He opened the glove compartment, took out a pack of cigarettes and had a smoke. He enjoyed the vista stretched out before him. For a long time now he had pondered how he could shake off Van Gogh's overwhelming influence. He was going to create something new out of the landscape and history of Iceland. These paintings would look like collaborations between Ensor and Van Gogh—Van Gogh in all his terrible anger and passion, Ensor with his wonderful, grotesque figures in a universe that seemed to be a carnival without end. Now the main thing was to get to the volcano, put up his easel and start the work.

He drove down the mountainside. The majestic volcano stood before him, twenty miles to the east. Suddenly he understood the day's task. In the year 1510 a farmer was riding past Mount Hekla with his wife and a hired hand when suddenly there was an eruption. The farmer, a man of legendary strength, covered his wife with turf and then the saddles of the horses. The horses disappeared into the burning black ash. The farmer's hair and clothing burned off but he made it to safety. He went back the following day to look for his wife. She was alive. The hired hand had suffocated to death. The horses were found alive but so badly burned they had to be put to sleep.

The farmer's heroic feat would be the day's task. Viktor could suddenly picture two horses running down the road, one on each side of the car, both of them on fire. Then the horses disappeared into the black ash he imagined hit the van with full force.

He drove as close to the base of the volcano as he could. The air was crystal clear at the peak. He opened the van, tossed his tent out onto the ground then took hold of his easel with great, tender care. The first order of business was to put up the tent and get everything organized.

Once he had done that, he made himself some soup. It was never good to paint on a full stomach but nor was there much to gain by working when starving—the objects in the painting might begin to resemble some tasty dish.

Suddenly a gust of wind blew off the mountain, where the sky rolled with tumultuous fury. He grabbed the box with his colors, put up the easel and got to work.

He let the paint drift this way and that on the canvas. He prayed to God to be able to paint a masterpiece, something he could be proud of, a painting good enough to place him among the major artists. No, better yet, a painting that would make him a master. A new Titian! A Bruegel! A Tintoretto! A masterpiece!

Now he could do nothing but work and wait and see what happened. A red spot, a green spot, a shape from the landscape, the hunchback of Mount Hekla. A horse began to appear—the horse was on fire. Should he try for the farmer and his wife? Van Gogh had been a great draftsman but still not as good as Picasso, who was the best.

He painted for almost two hours. It had gotten hot. Without him noticing, the wind had died down. He took off his sweater and his shirt and tossed them aside. He looked around and pictured the countryside turn into glowing ash. Three horses came running out of the firestorm; astride one of them was a man. Before Viktor knew it he had painted a contorted face right beneath the horse's tail, the head from the car accident. It was as if Francis Bacon had pitched in and added new life to the painting. Viktor felt all the joy and satisfaction of an artist who knows that he is on the correct path. A great painting was in the making.

"So here's an artist working out in nature just like the great Van Gogh used to," he heard someone say behind him.

He turned around to see an elderly couple, each holding a walking stick. Viktor was speechless. Was there not a moment's peace on this earth? Obviously these folks knew who he was. Was this Van Gogh stupidity going to haunt him for the rest of his days?

"What are you getting at?" Viktor muttered.

"Didn't he used to stand out in the countryside and paint?" the woman asked.

"I don't know anything about that," Viktor retorted.

"And who is the painter, if you don't mind me asking?" the man said.

"The name is Viktor," Viktor replied in anger. The reference to Van Gogh had been an accident. The couple had no clue who he was. And against all reason this angered him.

"We're art lovers, but I don't think we've ever heard of you," the man said, confirming Viktor's suspicion.

"But this is a very good painting," the woman said, eyeing the canvas.

"It's nowhere near finished," Viktor muttered. He was hoping the couple would leave.

"Well, let's move along, darling," the man said. "We're keeping the artist from working. We won't get up close to the mountain at the rate we're going."

"Where's your studio, in case we want to buy a painting, either for ourselves or as a gift for someone else?"

Viktor told them, feeling a bit more at ease. He didn't sell paintings all that often.

"We were thinking of something we could get at a cheap price," the woman added.

"Cheap?" Viktor replied with rising anger. "Then you should go someplace else."

He stood in front of the couple, naked from the waist up. He felt like a caricature of Kirk Douglas playing Vincent Van Gogh in that old movie. He was fifty-three years of age and the couple had never heard his name before! And when the woman had said "something we could get at a cheap price," he realized that intense anguish must have shown on his face. And before he knew it he had yelled, "Will you get out of my sight, you goddamn assholes!"

They stared at him. The man smiled wryly and looked at the painting and said, "The great Van Gogh would never have had a horse…"

"…defecate the head of a man," the woman said, finishing the remark.

"No, the great Vincent would never have put his name to something like that," the man added.

Viktor picked up a couple of stones and made as if he was going to throw them at the couple. They turned around and hurried away, towards Mount Hekla. He dropped the stones. In spite of the sun he felt cold. He put on his shirt and sweater and went into the tent to lie down and rest awhile.

"The great Vincent would never have put his name to something like that," the couple had said. Suddenly he felt strangely happy, almost elated. He hadn't felt so good for a long, long while.

❖ GAGA ❖

- OUTLAW OF MARS -

HE DECIDED TO CHANGE PLANETS AND WOKE UP ON MARS. THE room was in darkness, but he knew he was on Mars. He had chosen Mars because peace now reigned among the many warring nations of the red planet. He had really expected to have to find it in a spaceship or a flying saucer, and so he was rather surprised it had all been managed practically without effort.

He turned on the light and saw that he was in an exact replica of his room back on Earth. For a moment he regretted ever having set out on this journey, but it was too late to turn back now. He didn't find it surprising that the Martians had produced this imitation of his room. He had read that this was what they did on Mars if they didn't like a visitor. If anyone arrived uninvited they produced a facsimile of his childhood home and turned themselves into his mother, father, brothers and sisters. Then the guest was murdered in his sleep, just as he was beginning to think he was at home.

The Astronaut woke up properly. I've slept like a fool and given them a chance to murder me, it occurred to him. He sat up and touched the floor carefully with his feet. He looked towards the door. Would it open on one of those fearsome, Yok-Vombis catacombs of Mars, where black clothlike creatures fall down from the ceiling and wheel about the heads of astronauts and eat out their brains? He took his first strides and peeped out.

The hallway was familiar. A floorboard creaked in the same spot it did back on earth. He opened the bathroom door and turned on the light. My old electric razor must be in here somewhere, he thought. He opened the bathroom cabinet and there it lay in its usual place. There was a pair of scissors on the ledge underneath the mirror; they had even produced an imitation of the scissors. The Astronaut picked them up and looked at his reflection in the glass. He was nearly forty.

He cut off his beard, and then managed to remove nearly all his hair. He plugged in the razor and gave his face and scalp a long, thorough shave.

Then he took a step back and clenched his fist in front of his face. "Hail, O Earthman from Iceland on Terra," he said in a dark voice.

He bent near the mirror and examined himself carefully, turning his head from side to side. He saw that his eyes had acquired a distinctive setting in his face, that his cheeks looked fatter and his forehead had risen. "I'm a bit of a chubby chops with no hair," he murmured, "but at least now I ought to look spaced out enough for them all."

He went back to his room and quickly got his clothes on. He shut the door carefully and crept along the hallway, taking a big step in order to avoid placing his weight on the stair head, which he knew creaked.

He stole into the parlour and looked around him. The old grandfather clock still stood in its familiar place. It said seventeen minutes to six. It was getting on for morning on Mars. The Astronaut went over to the window and looked out at the street. It was all exactly as he would have expected. The streetlamp on the corner lit up the frozen expanse of white, and there was a gust of wind blowing a jet of snow off the house on the other side of the street.

He walked slowly around the parlour, examined the books, prodded the upholstery of the sofa, looked at the photographs of his relatives on the ledge above the radiator, the landscape paintings on the walls. He pinched the leaf of a potplant, and a crescent-shaped mark remained on it. He seized a small figurine from the table and shook it with all his might. He lifted the telephone receiver and listened to the dial tone. Then he got down on all fours and felt the pattern on the carpet. It was all incredibly true to life.

After a bit he got up and went along to his mother's bedroom door— she usually left it slightly open—and listened to her breathing. He went out to the coat rack and found his anorak. Then he put on his shoes, opened the front door and gasped in the cold air.

The pavements on Mars all seemed to have been sprayed with sheet ice. At first he slipped, but he quickly learned how to keep his balance.

How old was the red planet? The seas had dried up long ago— that was certain. And these buildings that were supposed to denote

Revkjavik! Where they stood it was easy to pick out the angular crystal towers rising up, stretching skyward and humming in the darkness. Some of them were several miles high, and they glowed with yellow and purple light. But this planet was dying. That was obvious, though it wasn't easy to say with any certainty when its decline had set in. The Astronaut guessed it must have been about three billion years ago. He was still immersed in these thoughts and feeling the cold terribly on his bare head when in the distance he caught sight of an old woman.

The street he was in was a long one, and to his left, on a high glass wall some several hundred yards long, there was a constant display of color pictures showing various eras in Martian history—the battles of the savage Therns, who were white and lived on human flesh, the eight-footed Thoats, those swift-moving giant yellow Martian lizards that were forever galloping at full tilt across the yellow Martian moss, roaring as they went, with those valiant green men on their backs, and there was His Highness the great Tars Tarkas, Jeddak of Thark, and there were pictures of the great naval and merchant fleets of Mars which had sailed the length and breadth of the planet before the seas had dried up, in the days when savoury white cheese and warm silkskin had been costly items of trade and commercial life on Mars had been booming. There were also pictures of the animal that ate sand and excreted bricks and had the habit of making pyramids, and the man-bird Tweel hopped along the glass wall and stood firmly on its beak in the red sand.

The Astronaut realized that Mars was a dying world where no help could be expected.

"I should have remembered that the Martians are past masters of optical illusion. They've produced this likeness of Reykjavik in self-defence," he thought. "That old woman could easily pass for an Icelandic charlady. She's amazingly lifelike. But what is she, really? Just an unusually clever Martian out for a walk, probably the same one who thought all this up."

The charlady drew closer. She was quite simply ridiculous in these surroundings. She wore a veil neatly tied under her chin, and she was clutching a plastic bag that was not only perished but had holes in it, and her shoes were in a worn down state. The Astronaut stood in the middle of the road with his feet planted wide apart. Opening both arms in a welcoming gesture, and dropping his jaw in astonishment, he viewed her fairly and squarely. Her eyes were watering in the fierce gale. A newspaper peeped from her plastic bag. She had to make a detour around him, and the Astronaut viewed her as she went. She had trouble in keeping her balance on the glass-smooth ice; now she had nearly disappeared in the white, swirling blizzard.

He looked up at the sky to see if it might not be possible to draw the Martian's attention to Earth, which is the third planet from the sun and known all over the universe by the name of Terra, but the sky was heavily overcast and the earth was nowhere to be seen. He couldn't resist following the poor woman.

"Now then, now then," he shouted, mockingly. "What a fine old woman you are, to be sure, going to your work so early in the morning to scrub for those rotten devils in Iceland, bah, bah, bah, haven't you got arthritis, too, and that's a really low-down stomach-turning disguise, you ought to be ashamed of yourself, you stupid woman." He ran in a wide circle around the woman and stuck both index fingers in his mouth. Suddenly angry, he went up to her, stamped on the ice and yelled: "Don't you ever get tired of this, don't you ever have enough of these cheap tricks, haven't you anything better to do than all this playacting nonsense, the way things are nowadays? But don't you worry, old girl," he shouted, clenching his fist at her. "I'll spread the news all over the universe, when I finally manage to catch a spaceship or a flying saucer out of here, that it's only fools and idiots who live here, who're prepared to turn a whole planet upside down just in order to be able to give refugees the nastiest possible reception, and now I'm going to take my leave of you, old woman, I hope you slip on the ice and break your hip and go to hell." The Astronaut was now so angry that he lost control of his voice and bawled these last words hoarsely.

"I'll get them to take you away, you crazy loony," said the old woman, shaking her fist at him. "I'll get them to take you away!" she screeched.

The Astronaut spent a long time wandering around the town. He was in a furious state of mind. In some of the streets the snow had melted and his feet started to get wet. It was a pity that everywhere he went there was something new and wonderful to be seen. If only he could have taken his time and enjoyed it.

All of a sudden he had an idea and stood still. "Maybe I ought to join in and play along with them. Then maybe they'll give up all this and drop their disguise. Perhaps the first thing I should do is go to a tailor's and get myself some decent clothes, made to measure, because that's the only thing they understand around here. There's not much point in trying to get to know the inhabitants of this planet unless you're dressed like a human being. But I'm flat broke! If I want to play their game I'll have to go home and get some money."

He was walking down a long street, and couldn't help admiring what a good likeness of Laugavegur it was. All the same, he took care to walk close to the walls of the houses and tested the ground before each step he took—you never knew whether one of those paving slabs might turn out to be the notorious revolving stone that spins a man around and hurls him into the bottomless ravines of Mars. He turned a corner and saw to his great relief that his mother wasn't up yet. He climbed the front steps and tried the door handle. The door was locked. Where am I going in such a hurry, he thought. He put his finger on the doorbell, but hesitated. Who knew what terrible monster might come to the door? It might be a bird woman with an iron nose a yard long and a single green eye and a coat of orange feathers—they were quite common on Mars. Or it might be the Princess of Helium. The beautiful ruler of the red men on a dying planet. All the same, he didn't feel like taking the risk, and he went back down onto the street again.

When he had lived on Terra he and his mother had run a small kiosk together. Here was a kiosk that was its exact replica. He went down the steps to the cellar, put his face to the window and looked in. Back home he would have had the place open by this hour. Packages of fresh newspapers were lying in the snow outside; in one place the wet had seeped in under the polythene. He picked up the packages and put them next to the wall of the kiosk. Then he tried the door, hut it too was locked. A man was coming down the street, and stopped behind him.

"Rognvaldur hasn't opened up yet," said the Martian. The Astronaut said nothing, did not even move his head. He felt about in the pocket of his anorak. There was a sheath knife in there.

The Martian moved closer and had a look. "Hey, Valdi, it's you, isn't it?" he said. "I hardly recognized you."

"Yes, it's me," said the Astronaut, without looking up.

"You've had a pretty good shave and haircut, haven't you?" said the Martian.

"It was time for it," said the Astronaut.

"Yes, I was wondering why you hadn't opened up when I came by earlier," said the Martian. "I was thinking of having myself one of your cigars."

"I overslept," said the Astronaut in an unsteady voice.

"Well, well, wouldn't it be a good idea if I had myself one of your cigars and put one in your own good mouth while I'm at it?" said the Martian.

"I'll take you and put you in my mouth if you're trying to take the mickey," said the Astronaut.

"My guess is you'd keel over if you did," said the Martian, who was short and fat, writhing from one foot to the other in sheer delight.

The Astronaut was silent.

When the Martian saw that the chat was at an end, he continued his way down the street, every now and again casting a glance back over his shoulder. The Astronaut watched him go and realized that he knew the man's prototype back on Earth. This was an incredibly good likeness of an Icelandic farmer called Gudmundur, a man who had a way with words. He had moved to Reykjavik and become involved in trouble and drinking. He was in the habit of coming into the kiosk to buy after-shave lotion and staying to talk for hours.

But here was the kiosk. And there was money in there. He was the only person in the street and the snow was as white as an inspiration from heaven. He struck the glass next to the door handle, but it didn't give. He struck it again, harder. He smashed it through. As he was clearing away the long, jagged shards of glass, some old putty came flaking out of the window frame. He picked up a lump of it and studied it closely. He felt inside and undid the latch. Then he went into the stuffy kiosk. Everything was just where it usually was. He opened the till and ripped the bills and receipts out of it until he came to a brown envelope. He opened the envelope and took out the bundle of banknotes inside. Now he could go into town and buy himself some decent clothes. Then the Martians would accept him and realize that all he wanted was to have somewhere to stay and to be allowed to live in peace among them.

He stuffed the money into the pocket of his anorak. Once again he walked up Laugavegur. He came to a large, brightly-lit shop window that held a display on men's clothing. Inside the shop a very elegantly clad Martian was arranging shirts in a row on a shelf. The Astronaut walked up and down in front of the shop window for a long time, observing the man inside.

Did he dare to go in? At last he summoned up his courage and opened the door.

The Martian looked up, but then went on with what he was doing.

"I want some clothes," said the Astronaut.

"What kind of clothes?" asked the Martian, full of suspicion.

"Smart clothes, friend," said the Astronaut. "Ha, ha, ha, I've decided I want you lot to like me."

"Very well," said the Martian, with a faint smile. "That's very sensible of you, if I may say so."

"Yes, I think so, too," said the Astronaut, and he began to stride around the shop from corner to corner.

"May I ask where you've come from?" said the Martian, giving him an appraising glance.

"I've been at sea," said the Astronaut. "Where do you think I've been? Mars? Ha, ha, ha." His laugh was a sarcastic one. "No, I've come off a trawler, friend. We came back with several hundred tons, you know. I've got a wad of notes this thick and now I want to get dressed up, see? We had a big catch. We were wrestling with the yellow one, friend. Wrestling with the yellow one in a force twenty gale and cold and burning frost and filth."

He didn't like trotting out this rubbish, and he expected the Martian to give a howl and turn into a five-yard-tall Thorn, waving his long hands, on which each fingernail is capable of turning into a sharp dagger if required. But nothing happened. The Martian went on running his men's outfitting shop in Reykjavik. He showed the Astronaut the jackets he had in stock; there was a long row of them. Everything in the shop was suffused in brilliant light. The Astronaut looked at himself in a full length mirror. He didn't think his shaven head went well with his anorak.

Within a short space of time he had selected a really splendid-looking yellow suit and a warm blue overcoat. He bought a pair of red leather shoes, a white shirt and a brightly-coloured bow tie. He rummaged in the pile of his old clothes and found the wad of banknotes, his dark glasses, his house keys and the sheath knife.

"I've got a knife here," said the Astronaut, putting it down on the counter.

"Oh yes?" said the Martian.

"I want something to put it in."

"Oh, we don't sell anything of that kind," said the Martian, stiffly.

"I can't just carry it about in my pocket like that," said the Astronaut.

No, I can see that, sir," said the Martian, and he peered around the shop. "I haven't got any sheaths," he said after a while.

"How about a case, then?" The Astronaut looked around and caught sight of some cases on a shelf up near the ceiling. Back home on Earth these were called director's cases. "Give me one of those."

"A whole case just for one knife?" asked the Martian.

"What's so funny about that?"

"Oh, nothing, really," said the Martian. "It's just a bit unusual, that's all. I'm not accustomed to people wanting a case just for one knife;

anyway, this one here is very well made." He fetched a stepladder and took down one of the cases. "It's made in Spain, real leather, none of your cheap plastic junk." He snapped open the silver-plated hasps so that the lid sprang up; the case was padded with black silk on the inside. The Astronaut placed the knife in the center of the case and watched it sink into the soft silk. Then the Martian locked the case and went over to the till.

"Thank you, sir," he said as he opened the door. "Just a minute, though," he added, when the Astronaut was already outside on the pavement. "What am I to do with your old clothes?"

"Throw them away if you like."

"I think I'd rather donate them to a museum," said the Martian with a smile, and he closed the door.

The Astronaut went to the shop window and looked in. He was hoping that now Mars was going to change. He was hoping he would now look through the window and see one of the enormous dives of the red planet where men and women lie stoned out of their minds on dirty couches under the yellow light of the Shanga-lamps and let the rays turn them into sabre-toothed tigers and fearsome black lions. But nothing happened. The Martian, who had resumed arranging his row of shirts, looked out at him and raised his eyebrows inquisitively.

The Astronaut gave up and walked into the center of town, talking out loud to himself about the clothes shop he had just visited. The sky had begun to grow light. He walked energetically, with broad strides, swinging the case and listening to the sheath knife rattling about inside.

The center of town reminded him of some sickly-sweet Christmas card. The clock on the central square said eleven minutes past ten. He went into the airline office and brought a flight ticket. He walked around Lækjartorg, swinging his case and looking up at the sky for a long time, but the earth was nowhere to be seen. He could only see Phobos and Deimos, the two hurtling moons of Mars. He took up a position in the center of the square, put on his dark glasses and looked searchingly about him. The Martians passed to and fro without paying him any attention.

He put his hand over his heart to make it plain that he had come in peace; he had read that this was the custom on Mars. He bowed in all directions and said "Kaor"—the Martian greeting—in a soft, clear voice, but no emissary came to bid him welcome to the red planet.

He strode on down Austurstræti and looked at the houses on either side of the street. "How can I prove to them that I'm from Earth?" he wondered. "I couldn't even construct a food mixer, not even on pain of death, and it's a common enough gadget. And what's Somalia? I feel I know the name, but I can't remember whether it's a mountain or a country. I should have brought an encyclopedia with me and shown these idiots what a remarkable place the Earth is. But what good would that have done? You don't find everything in encyclopedias, and they'd just have said I was a salesman."

On he strode, and every now and again he shouted "Barsoom, Barsoom, Tyrr, Tyrr," in order to let it be known that he was able to say "Mars" in two of the Martian tongues. He looked from passer-by to passer-by and laughed an ironic, mocking laugh, but only two or three of them gave him a curious glance, and a few boys selling newspapers put their heads together and whispered and giggled.

The Astronaut suddenly felt himself trembling with a sense of impotence. Changing planets was quite a struggle. Maybe I ought to go home to mother, he thought. After all, I did break a window, and that will never do, ha ha. They may just as easily send an emissary to greet me if I wait quietly on the side somewhere. They probably need time to get their bearings. It can't be every day that a refugee arrives on Mars from another planet. As he walked past the Salvation Army hostel it occurred to him that there was one place in Reykjavik that was always relatively deserted at this hour, and where it would be easy for them to find him when they wanted to. He could wait there in safety. It was only a short distance away. He was going in the right direction for it. There was the old cemetery. He strode up Sudurgata, swinging his director's case, and was the first person to enter the cemetery that day. The snow was smooth and tranquil.

But this was no dream. He was on Mars. He swept the snow away and sat down on a grave slab where there was a good view, put his case to one side and had a look at Revkjavik. There was Tjornin, the Lake, where it ought to be. It was gleaming in the winter sun and the Astronaut could see some boys skating on it. He waited, hut nobody came. He could imagine all the multifarious life that seethed beneath the roofs of those houses. A meeting of the Supreme Council would be taking place to discuss him, the wisest philosophers of Mars would have arrived from every corner of the planet, green men from the dried-up seabeds and Therns from the terrible valley of Dor that lies in the foothills of the yellow mountains of Mars.

Why don't I just set fire to Reykjavik? thought the Astronaut. Mars is a waterless planet, so they won't be able to put the flames out. He looked at the roofs of the houses and set fire to them one after the other. He watched the flames leaping from roof to roof, windowpanes burst in the heat and black smoke rolled out in a flood of sparks, everything became a mad stampede around him, Revkjavik was burning, and black rafters were hurtling down into the foundations of the buildings. And when the city had burned to the ground the red planet began to reveal its inner self. He saw Mars rise up from the ground—eight-turreted purple and yellow crystal towers, several hundred yards broad on each side, reared up from the hillside along the Lake, pushing aside the blackened rafters and rising with a steady tintinnabulation towards the sky. There they stood, humming. This was the red planet.

The Astronaut moved over on his slab, crossed his legs and leaned against a tree trunk. He felt the cold from the tree penetrate his body through his new coat. "I'm here and nowhere else," said the Astronaut aloud to himself.

He was getting fed up with waiting. How long was he going to have to sit crouching here? From time to time he felt himself nodding off to sleep, and then he would dream something or another. He remembered one of the dreams: he was back home on Earth and was standing waiting at the airport. He didn't know what for. Eventually a man came along—in the dream he knew that this man was dead—and handed him a painting. The painting was wrapped up in brown paper and tied firmly with string. Then the man said something that was really very funny. The Astronaut woke up bursting with laughter, but try as he might he could not remember what it was that had been so funny. He had only dozed off for a moment. It was still broad daylight on Mars.

He waited for it to get dark. From time to time he had to get up and walk about and beat the warmth back into himself with his arms. It was just as well his overcoat was so thick. A grey pigeon came in to land, furling its wings and swaying in flight. It alighted on the branch of a tree; the branch rocked beneath its weight. It hopped onto another branch, sending the snow showering down in flakes. The pigeon rocked on the branch, looking stiffly into the wind. Its wings were immaculate!

A truck went by and the Astronaut caught a clear view of the blue driver's cabin over the cemetery wall. He heard the sound of the gate opening, and an old woman appeared on the path. She went up to a nearby grave and began to dust the snow off the stone. She was carrying a string bag, and from it she took a plastic container of liquid cleaner, a brush and a stiff floor cloth which she wet in the snow and then started to clean the gravestone with. The Astronaut stayed where he was and watched her. He gathered some snow in his hands, stood up, formed an iron-hard snowball and approached the old woman. He offered her the snowball, letting it lie in his outstretched palm. The woman looked at him in surprise.

"This is all made of the Earth, isn't it?"

The woman said nothing.

"This is all made of the Earth, isn't it?" said the Astronaut, sarcastically, tossing the snowball up and down as he spoke.

"I suppose so, my boy," said the old woman.

"Well, it's what you want me to think, isn't it?" said the Astronaut, puffing himself up. "But I'm not from Earth." He began to adopt a formal mode of address towards the old woman, laughing all the while. "Who told you that, may I ask? Ha, ha, whoever told you that was a liar, my dear lady, I was born and brought up here, I'll have you know, ha, ha, ha."

"Oh, I'd never dream of arguing with you," said the woman.

"I'm from Mars," said the Astronaut. He waited, smiling sarcastically and giving the old woman an attentive stare.

"Well, you're travelling around, I'll say that much for you," said the woman.

"So you're just going to go on as before?"

"That I am," said the old woman.

"I am now above God," said the Astronaut, after a brief silence.

"Yes, well, in that case I think I'd better be off home," said the woman. "I don't like the idea of standing here having a chat with someone who's above God."

The Astronaut sat down on his case. It had begun to get dark. The woman finished cleaning the gravestone and went away. On the hill along the Lake streetlights were going on. He sat there, stiff with cold, in the darkness. It was starting to snow again, and he watched the flakes melting on his hands and piling up on his blue overcoat. His hands were unable to melt the snow fast enough. The Astronaut sat motionless and let his head sag on his chest, open-mouthed.

- THE WAR OF THE WORLDS -

AT LAST HE GOT TO HIS FEET AND LET THE SNOW FALL OFF HIM. HE stroked his bald head and stamped his feet. Then he picked up the case, knocked it against the tree, and went out of the cemetery. He walked for a long time without thinking about anything at all and without knowing where he going. He grew warmer as he walked. A wind was getting up and small whirlwinds of snow were chasing about the streets. He made a mental effort to recall the map of the red planet so as to form some notion of his whereabouts and guessed that he was somewhere in the Valles Marineris. Olympus Mons, the largest volcano in the solar system, was not very far away. But now he had suddenly reached the end of the street and he looked with anguish ahead of him. What he could see was the sea. There was a great commotion of waves and the sea foaming white in the darkness. He caught a glimpse of seagulls swooping along the shore in the heavy snow. The Astronaut began to walk along the shore. To be quite honest, he had not really bargained on coming across a sea on Mars. He had observed that the Martians found it an easy matter to produce one little lake and make it snow, but this bawling pressure of water that raged before him was quite simply incredible.

What had he known about the sea when he had lived on Terra? Not much. He knew that in some places it was very deep, and that life had begun in it, but how it had come into existence he couldn't remember. Where was Earth now, anyway? He looked up at the sky but couldn't see it anywhere, even though he stood for a long time searching for it. All he could see was the moon Phobos, hurtling in from the sea like a yellow potato and hissing over the town.

He walked some two hundred yards along the shore, but there was no parting of the waters. Maybe it'll shift aside if I walk towards it without hesitating, he thought, and he began to stumble down the frozen white boulders of the shore. A smacking wave sprayed over him, and the Astronaut was wet through, tasting salt when he licked his lips.

He used the case to support himself as he straightened himself up, and peered into the seething waves. Then he turned quickly away from the sea and walked along Vesturgata into the town. A cat came out of a gateway and picked its way cautiously over the melting snow that lay in the street. It was heading for the pavement on the other side. This nonsense must stop, thought the Astronaut when he saw the cat. I'll have to talk to them. But I've tried that, and it's no good. I must at least try to eavesdrop on them, find out what they're saying to one another, for it may well be that they can only talk to aliens in allegories. Maybe if I listen hard enough they'll send me a message that way.

He arrived in midtown and went into the Central Café, where he took a seat in a corner. He ordered a hamburger and French fries and a large glass of orange fizz, but he didn't touch any of it even though he was hungry and thirsty and hadn't had anything to eat or drink since his arrival on Mars. He turned up the collar of his new coat, felt in one of its pockets, found his dark glasses and put them on. He looked around him, pricking his ears up. A waitress came by, calling in a loud voice:

"Who was it who wanted cold pilsner? Who was it who wanted ice cold pilsner?"

Two Martians were sitting at the next table drinking coffee. He forgot what they were for a moment; they so much resembled ordinary Icelanders that he almost took a liking to them. One of them looked at the Astronaut with a faint smile, and then said to his companion:

"You'd almost suppose the whole of Reykjavik was at a fancy dress ball."

The Astronaut gave a start. Now they had more or less admitted that Reykjavik was nothing but an illusion, and that was half the battle.

"That you would," said the other, after a long silence.

"So you're moving away from town?"

"That's right."

"Where to?"

"Up north, I decided to do it a long time ago. They're pleading for me up there. Prepared to do anything for me. It was stupid of me ever to have wasted my time wandering around down here in the South. If I'd had the sense to go up north right at the beginning I'd never have gotten into any trouble. You can't make mistakes at moments like that. That was where I went wrong. It's absolutely essential to deal with things like that at the very outset. Take your business to the right people." He cast a sidelong glance at the Astronaut.

"Yes, that's true. A man can lead a secure life up north," said the other. "It's a fine place, but I'm from the Islands, remember."

"Yes, so you are," said the man who had spoken first. "You're from the Islands."

The Vestmann Islands, thought the Astronaut. Perhaps if I'd had the courage to walk into the sea it would all have gone like clockwork? But I'm soaking wet. What were the northern regions of Mars called? He could remember the name of one of them. Vastitas Borealis.

The two men left a newspaper behind on the table. The Astronaut pushed his dark glasses forward on his nose and looked to see if anyone was watching him; then he grabbed the paper. He read for over two hours while his clothes dried, but he could find nothing hidden between the lines that seemed to have anything to do with himself. His head was aching now, and he had broken out in a cold sweat from the exertion. Up north! If I'd had the sense to go up north right at the beginning I'd never have got into any trouble. That was what the Martian had said, and the other man had agreed with him. That must be the message. It couldn't be anything else.

He crossed the Central Square, stooping forwards in the sleet. A long line of cars was on its way out of town, and he stuck out his hand and held it there until a taxi came along.

"Well, here we are then," said the Astronaut, getting into the back seat.

"Very well, my friend," said the taxi driver. "And where are we going?"

"You ought to know that," said the Astronaut. "You've got special permission to be here."

"No, I'm afraid I've no idea," said the taxi driver, taking a look at the Astronaut in the driving mirror.

"I know everything about Mars," said the Astronaut. "I know that its year lasts six-hundred eighty-seven days and that its mass is six-point-four times ten to the twenty-third tons."

"Well, you're all right then, aren't you, my friend? Ha, ha, ha," said the taxi driver, laughing loudly.

"What's the biggest volcano here, friend, can you tell me that?" asked the Astronaut.

"Well, now, wouldn't it be Hekla?" said the taxi driver after he had thought for a while.

"I know your game," said the Astronaut, who was quite beside himself by this time, and he hammered his fist on the seat-back in front of him. "No, it's Olympus Mons, which is three times the height of Mount Everest. It's bigger in area than Iceland on Terra, and it's the highest mountain here on Tyrr and the biggest volcano in the whole solar system, and still active."

"Where do you want me to drive to?" asked the taxi driver.

"Out of town," said the Astronaut. He sat stiffly in the back seat with his chin on the case and watched the town going by.

They had travelled a good way along the Western Highway when the Astronaut said imperiously:

"Take me to Hekla."

"You won't get a living soul to take you there in this weather, the roads are all closed out east," said the taxi driver, and he pulled up at the side of the road.

"Who is it sitting at the wheel?" wondered the Astronaut. "I ought to cut his throat. I ought to cut his throat and see what's really there, underneath. Maybe it's a holy Thern in a yellow wig, wearing the distinctive headdress that denotes rank among the Therns. One of the holy princes of Mars from the golden mountains that tower above the mysterious and horrible Valley of Dor from which no man returns alive." He put the case down, open, on the front seat.

"Wouldn't you like to go home and lie down, friend?" said the taxi driver.

"Observe that I have a knife, O holy Thern."

"I see it, friend."

"I don't give a damn about Hekla," said the Astronaut in a shrill, excited voice, stamping his feet on the floor of the cab. "Olympus Mons is the highest volcano here! Do you hear? Olympus Mons!" The Astronaut thumped the seat-back in front of him with balled fists, over and over again.

"Well, if you say so, friend," said the taxi driver.

The Astronaut found some money and threw it to the Martian, picked up his case, got out and slammed the door. The taxi made a U-turn and disappeared. The Astronaut watched it disappear in the blizzard. He buttoned his coat up to the neck and struggled several hundred yards up the road in his slippery shoes with the wind in his face. Once he stepped over the edge of the road and there was a cracking of tall, frozen grass. He was hoping he would walk out of the snowstorm into sun and summer; he was hoping he would see the snowstorm as a white cliff behind him, would feel the soft, yellow moss beneath his feet and see the strange vegetation that is so characteristic of Mars, see the majestic Olympus Mons towering miles into the sky; he even expected to come across a hothouse full of large, pale eggs—the women on Mars lay eggs—but it didn't happen. He stood still and listened to the howling of the storm and looked into the bottomless darkness. It had all been a lie: there was nothing in the north, nothing but an endless road into blizzards and darkness. He turned on his heel and walked back into the town.

Every so often he peered up at the sky; it was not until some two hours later that he regained any sense of his whereabouts. He was walking down a long street. The wind had died down, and it had stopped snowing. If he had been on Earth he would have guessed he was somewhere in the Thingholt district of Reykjavik in the middle of the night. He stopped suddenly and looked about him. He studied the houses, one after the other. An icicle was hanging from a pipe that ran down from a roof gutter; he gave the icicle a smack with the case, and it broke off and fell into the snow and disappeared. What had he done to upset these people? Why had they put it into his head to take a taxi out of their town? Why couldn't they leave him be? It was true that Mars was only half the size of Earth, but there were no seas on Mars, and so there ought to be more than enough room for everyone. "I'll show them I'm capable of getting my own back," he said out loud. "I'll give them something to think about. I'll kill one of them. Martians respect the martial spirit." He quickened his pace, filled with sudden fear at this new idea. He shook the case and listened to the rattling inside.

He was standing in front of a majestic, three-story stone house, the outer walls of which were covered in marling. There was no light in any of the windows. He looked at the house and then at the iron gate and felt his heart surging fast and evenly. He seized the latch and opened the gate and climbed the steps to the front door slowly and cautiously. A lamp shone above the steps. There were two doors to choose from. He peered in at a window and found himself looking into a dimly-lit vestibule in which there was a portrait of some bearded fellow in a sou'wester smoking a pipe. A Finnish sledge stood propped against the wall. There were gloves on the radiator and beneath the radiator various items of footwear, including a pair of large wading boots. He peeped through the next window but could not see anything—there was a crocheted curtain in the way. He tried the door handle, but the door was firmly locked. There was a faint glow of electric light under the doorbell, and the Astronaut could hear a humming sound; he bent over and put his ear to the illuminated rectangular doorbell. The hum was emanating from there. He grasped the door handle again and gave the door a violent shake, but although it rattled in its jambs, it remained firmly locked. He put the case down in the snow on the front steps, picked up the knife and tried to force the door open with it, but to no avail. Pieces of wood came away from the doorframe. He put the knife back in the case and felt a strange sense of impotence. Shakily he descended the steps and waded through the snow around the corner of the house and into the garden. He bent down and examined one of the basement windows; it was locked. He saw that one of the brackets was loose and the window was warped. He tried to get the knife inside and prise the other bracket loose, but the gap was too narrow and it didn't work. There was a staircase down to the basement door. He went down the stairs and seized hold of the door handle—the door was unlocked. It seemed to open onto endless space. He crept inside and found himself in a hot laundry room. There was an old sofa against one of the walls, and he slumped onto it for a while, rocking to and fro with his case in his arms, waiting until he had thawed out.

He sprang to his feet, took off his overcoat and laid it on the sofa. He opened the door. There was a staircase there. It led up, into the house. He listened as hard as he could, but could hear nothing, and went into the hallway. A new-looking bicycle stood there. One of his trouser legs caught on a pedal and the bicycle slid down the wall to end in a twisted, tangled heap on the floor. The Astronaut stood in deathly quiet with his mouth half open; he hung his head and listened. The noise was like that of an explosion. It leapt up the staircase, reverberated from wall to wall, passing from floor to floor, and finally bursting up through the ventilator shaft to expand like some strange flower and remain there in frozen silence. He began to climb the stairs, arrived at a door, opened it and found himself in the vestibule, on the inside of the crocheted curtains this time. The stairs continued upwards. He climbed them two at a time, but got out of breath and had to sit down and rest on a soft curve in the staircase. He sat dead still, and rested. Five or ten minutes, reckoned by Earth-time, went by. Then he got to his feet and continued to stride up the stairs two at a time until he came to another door. There was a name on it. It was an Icelandic one. Árni Palsson. The name was engraved on a gold plate, and beneath it was the word "Electrician." Electrician! The Astronaut could not restrain a giggle. He swayed backwards on the doormat and looked at the name. Electrician! Those poor wretches back home on Earth!

Then, however, he donned a stern expression and opened the door. He found himself in the entrance hall. There was a mirror with a gilded and ornamented frame; under the mirror there was a telephone on a ledge and a rococo chair beside it. A tube of lipstick lay on the ledge. He removed its gold top and screwed up the stick. It was red. The Astronaut began to paint his face all over with great conscientiousness. When he had finished painting his throat, face and shaven head he picked up a hand mirror from the ledge and coloured the back of his neck. Now he looked like one of the red men of Mars. Now he looked like one of the inhabitants of Helium, the capital city of the red men. Now no one on Mars would notice that he was from another planet. He could smell the sickly sweet odor from his face. He got to his feet and looked into the parlour and out through the window; he could see the floodlit building of the University of Iceland in the darkness. Reykjavik was still out there. He sat down again and looked at himself in the mirror. What were most striking were the white eyes in the glowing red face. The eyes squinted slightly. Every pore was visible. He sat in the chair for a long time and waited for someone to telephone and announce a truce, but no call came. All at once he was overcome by an irresistible desire to call someone up himself. Call any number and see who answered, find out how far it extended this network of playacting. He lifted the receiver and dialed a number at random. Eagerly, he waited. He could see that the telephone cable led into the lost Carrion Caves of Mars, where the holy and ferocious Apt keeps watch; to the Carrion Caves, the only land route to the city of Okar at the Martian North Pole. After a while a woman's newly awoken voice came on the line and said "Hello."

"Hello," whispered the Astronaut.

"Who am I talking to?" asked the voice.

"You know that as well as I do," said the Astronaut. "After all, you're taking part in all this." He continued to whisper.

"Who is this?" asked the voice.

"You know very well who I am," said the Astronaut, mockingly.

"Is that you, Siggi?" said the voice, which had finished waking up now.

"No," said the Astronaut. "My name's not Siggi. Don't give me that. I know your game."

"Yes, it is you," said the woman, who was wide awake now.

"No," said the Astronaut. "I'm the visitor from Terra."

"What do you mean ringing me up at this hour with your impudent nonsense?" said the voice. "I was fast asleep."

"You're the one who's impudent, not me," said the Astronaut.

"Me?" said the voice, trembling. "Me, impudent? After the way you've behaved?"

"And how have I behaved?" asked the Astronaut.

"You know perfectly well," said the voice.

"How?" asked the Astronaut.

"You know how," said the voice, which was close to tears.

"No, I've no idea how I've behaved," said the Astronaut. "It was you who started it. There's enough room here."

"Have you any idea," said the voice, full of furious hatred. "Have you any idea what I think of you?"

"No," said the Astronaut. "I don't want anything special, I..."

"So you don't want anything special?" hissed the voice. "What about me, what do you think I've been through, how can you dare to talk to me, you monster, I want to be rid of you," sobbed the voice. "You've no right to talk to me like this, you ought to be killed for it. But I'll tell you one thing," said the voice decisively. "I've always known that you're scared, scared, that you're a coward, a coward..."

"The seas have dried up, there's enough room here," whispered the Astronaut.

"What?"

"I said the seas have dried up, there's enough room on Mars."

"Don't you ever ring me up with nonsense like this again," said the voice. "Never, never."

And the receiver was slammed down.

The red man hung up cautiously and got to his feet. He went into the parlor. It was divided into two and a crocheted bell cord hung on a broad doorframe. In the middle of the floor of the left partition stood an oval-shaped mahogany table. There was a green crystal bowl on the table and under the bowl lay a crocheted tablecloth; moonlight was shining onto the table, touching the bowl and making its moulded glass glitter with a green brilliance so that the table sparkled in the radiance from Deimos, the second of the rapidly orbiting moons of Mars now passing over the town in the direction of the house, until he thought it was going to tear the roof off—it was ten times the size of the Earth's moon—and which then disappeared. In the parlour there were shelves made of dark wood, stuffed with books, and heavy carved chairs beside a coffee table. In one corner stood a cupboard full of porcelain figures—frozen dancing couples and a little girl reading a book.

There were two doors to choose from. He opened one of them cautiously and tiptoed inside. He could hear the sound of breathing in the darkness. He got down on his hands and knees, opened the case and took out the knife. He crept right up to the bed. Bending forwards to take a look at the bed, he saw a face. This Martian was an old woman. Her head lay small and frail on the pillows; her mouth was half open and her breathing came in short gasps. The expression on her face was a tortured one; it seemed as though this Martian was having bad dreams. "Why don't I just take the knife to her and finish her off?" thought the Astronaut. "Sink it into this old carcass and watch it disappear in a flash and see a black Martian crab writhing on the pillow, squirting poison from its broken shell. Then I'll have penetrated their disguise and Reykjavik will come toppling down. The illusion will vanish. And when I've killed one of them they'll be compelled to take me seriously and drop all this fooling around and welcome me."

The moon Phobos, which had completed its orbit, shot past the window, and the face on the pillow was clearly visible.

"No," said the Astronaut. "This isn't a worthy opponent. If I murder this one, they'll think I'm a weakling, for they're all heroes here, and Mars is the planet of the god of war." He picked up the case and stole cautiously out of the room. Then he put the case down on the parlor floor, went to the next door, and pushed it gently.

He looked into a bedroom. There was a double bed in there. A man and a woman lay asleep in it. On the woman's side of the bed there was a small crib. He crept back into the parlour and began to move things around. He moved a flower vase, an ashtray, a box of matches, he pushed one of the pictures out of alignment. He was hoping that the illusion would burst, that the walls would go flying in every direction, and he would see that he was really on top of one of the great abandoned buildings of Mars where there is nothing to fear except the terrible white apes that dwell there and are the most fearsome animals in the whole universe, have four arms and are more than five yards tall—but nothing happened. He went back to the parlour table and sat down. He moved the crystal bowl. He began to pick at the crochet work of the tablecloth with the fingers of his right hand. The table was black and shiny. He worked his finger through the crocheted pattern, taking more and more of the cloth in his hand. And then he heard a clock strike. It was a clock on the top floor of the house, and it gave out a deep, golden chiming. He waited and counted. Four. Shortly afterwards a child began to cry in the bedroom. It was a very young child. The Astronaut could see the woman resting her head on one arm and leaning forwards. Her long hair flowed down into the crib. But the child did not stop crying. Then he heard singing. The voice that sang was a gentle one, and it sang so beautifully and with so much love that he could see tall grass swaying in a warm breeze, as if a hand were caressing a large field back home on Earth. The voice sang:

> *Sleep, sleep my son.*
> *The seal is asleep in the sea,*
> *The swan on the breaker,*
> *the seagull on the hill,*
> *the cod in the deep water.*
> *Sleep, I love you.*
>
> *The cow in the stall,*
> *the calf in the yard,*
> *the hart on the moor,*
> *in the sea the fish,*
> *the mouse under the stone,*
> *the worm in the earth,*
> *the snake in the stones.*
> *Sleep, I love you.*
>
> *The beaver by the lake,*
> *the cormorant in the cliffs,*
> *the fox in his lair,*
> *the trout in the lake,*

the swan on the ice,

the duck on the riverbank,

Sleep, I love you.

Bull seals on the flats,

Cow seals in the sound,

the bear in its hide,

with broad paws,

the wolf in the willow,

and the pike in the lake,

the eel in the pool,

Sleep, I love you.

There was nothing he could tell them about Earth. They knew it all. This was a song that contained nearly the whole planet. There was Terra from Iceland to the Galapagos Archipelago. Sleep, sleep my son. He listened to the sounds that were coming from the bedroom, straining his ears. The child must have fallen asleep. Sleep, sleep my son. He dozed at the table with his hand on the knife.

- THE SILENT CITY -

THE ASTRONAUT CAME TO WITH A START, AND FOR A FEW MOMENTS he thought he was back home on Earth. He had had a dream but had forgotten it immediately on waking. He looked around him and remembered he was on Mars; and so overwhelmed by anguish was he that he could not move his head, no matter how hard he tried. He thought the moment would never pass. I'll have to watch I don't go crazy, he thought.

At last he looked out of the window and saw it was still pitch dark. What had the Martian been singing? An Icelandic lullaby? Hadn't his mother used to sing that song once upon a time? Sleep, sleep my son. It was understandable that he should be a complete outlaw on this planet, but why these tortures? Why hadn't they just put him in the runaway booths or driven him out into the sands? If the Martians want war they can have it, thought the Astronaut, filled with hatred. He got down on all fours with the knife, but then he changed his mind, raised himself on one knee and placed the knife in the crystal bowl on the table without making a sound.

He began to crawl over the carpet. He pushed at the door with his bald head, leaving a red patch on it as it soundlessly glided open on the darkness. Now there was cold linoleum beneath his hands. He crawled up to the crib and then lay face down on the linoleum, which smelled of floor-polish. He turned over on his side and laid his forehead against one of the crib's hard, cold legs. The air in the room was heavy with sleep. He began to listen to the breathing and could hear that one of the Martians was snoring quietly but evenly through a blocked nose. The Astronaut lay still, waiting for his heart to stop beating so violently. Then he raised himself on one elbow and peeped through the bars of the crib. He put his hand inside the crib and felt the warm chest and the face of the child.

After a while the Astronaut crept out and found his director's case. A pink hat hung on a hook above the coat rack. He tried the hat on in various poses and thought it went rather well with his red face. He positioned the hat firmly on his bald head and closed the door carefully behind him. On the ground floor a strip of light was shining into the entrance hall, illuminating the coarse material of the doormat. A newspaper was sticking through the letter box. Dawn had begun to break once more on the red planet. He sat down on the stairs with the case in his lap. He was about to take out the knife when he remembered that he had left it in the bowl on the table upstairs; for some reason he was unable to make himself go back up there to get it. He knew that the upper floor of the house would have changed by now. That large windows were now gaping at the two moons, that the light of Deimos was falling over the broad stone floors, and that two giant white apes now lay in the double bed. In a short while they would waken in their lair and smell the odour of Earth, see that their offspring was dead, and set up a horrible shrieking. They would run crazily from hall to hall of this Martian labyrinth in search of the alien from Terra. He rested against the wall and listened to the voices. He couldn't make out what they were saying.

Suddenly the hallway was flooded with light and a little girl who looked about five years old came running out and snatched the newspaper from the letter box without noticing him. The letter box sprang shut with a bang and she ran back inside. The Astronaut could hear them talking. He could see strong mouths moving and producing words.

"Are you going to fetch the girl?"

"Can't you do it?"

"No, I promised I'd go and visit Dad."

"Why can't your sister go, you've got a sister, haven't you?"

"Mum, I want some toast."

"No, you're not having any more."

"I want some toast and jam."

"No, you're not having any more, you've had two slices already."

"I want toast and jam! I want toast!"

"For God's sake, woman, give the child its bread, will you?"

"Give it to her yourself, it'll be your fault if she bursts."

"Rubbish, she's not too fat. This fine little girl isn't too fat. Daddy's little girl isn't too fat."

The Astronaut felt unable to listen to any more of this, so he went straight into the hallway and opened the door to the cellar without looking into the kitchen. He went quickly down the stairs, feeling the house alter behind him as he went. He jumped over the bicycle. Above him he could hear the doors opening, a loud voice shouting "Árni, Árni!" and a heavy tread coming down the hall.

"Anna!" shouted a voice. "Anna! Is that you, Anna?" and the Astronaut heard a hissing sound. In the middle of the staircase stood one of the blue, one-eyed plant men who have a sucker on the palm of each hand, and whom the Therns call upon with their horrible screams to murder the trusting souls who have set off on their final journey down the terrible river Iss in the Valley of Dor. These plant men of Mars provide themselves with food by running their hands over trees and bushes and shaving their leaves off.

The plant man took another step closer.

The Astronaut looked around him.

"Is there somebody down there?" he heard a voice shout. "Hallo!"

Beside the sofa on which he had rested the night before stood an old, rickety-legged table piled with tools of various kinds and rusty nails and screws in jars. There were old cans of paint with splashes of hardened paint on them. A rusty-headed axe lay there.

He heard the sound of treading feet and finally the door was shut.

"Since they've got my knife I'll take their axe," thought the Astronaut, and he opened the case and put the axe down on the silk inside. Everything in proportion, he said to himself.

He put on his coat again, went resolutely over to the cellar door, opened it and looked out. It was still completely dark and Reykjavik hadn't changed. The snow was giving off an intense radiance; grey clouds were scudding across the sky. In the garden a large tree was swaying in the wind. Trickles of water running down its bark made the trunk black and shiny.

The Astronaut walked quickly down into the garden, hid behind the tree, and looked up at the house. He expected to see at one glance that it was built of those sturdily hewn rocks that are so characteristic of the Martian architecture of old, he expected to see one of those abandoned, windowless buildings of the fourth planet, but the Martians wouldn't give in and meet him, even though he had killed one of them. He looked in through a lit-up window. An extravagant chandelier with drop-shaped glass ornaments hung from the ceiling.

He strode knee-deep in snow further down into the garden. He came to a high wall. Panting, he climbed onto it, hurting his stomach on its sharp crest. The upper part of the wall was slippery with sheet ice. He hurled the case down the other side and watched it slide obliquely down a frozen snowbank. It came to rest in a soft drift. The Astronaut heaved his other leg over, but then fell off the wall unceremoniously and struck his cheek on the glass-hard snowbank. He heard a roaring noise in his head, and he made a silent cry of pain. He got up, straightened his hat, picked up the case, dusted the snow off it, and walked off down the lane between the houses. A girl with flying blond hair was standing there on a high stone stairway; she was wearing a white coat that billowed out in the wind and she looked at him in surprise.

The Astronaut walked quickly past her and down a path lined with twisted trees. He banged the gate shut after him and the girl turned to watch him go. Walking and running by turns, he passed the Concert Hall and arrived at Fríkirkjuvegur. He looked out at the lake and saw that a thaw was setting in—puddles had formed on the surface of the ice. He could see some older floes several inches below the layer of transparent ice. He came to some ducks that were asleep on the ground. With short, stomping steps he walked towards them, never hesitating, and they woke up and waddled one after the other onto the lake. He turned into Vonarstraeti and looked up at the clock on the Cathedral tower. It was exactly half past seven in the morning. Long rows of frozen vehicles stood along both sides of Tjarnargata. One of them was a van and he walked around it in circles with large strides, several times. He walked the whole length of Tjarnargata without meeting a soul. Wet, black branches were waving in the easterly gale, and he was beginning to get a bad ache in his left ear. He turned into Skothusvegur and stood on the lake bridge, leaning against the railings and pointing to a dustcart that was getting into difficulties on the slope. He lowered his head, looked rhythmically to right and to left, and made another circular tour of the Lake without anything noteworthy happening.

He arrived back at the bridge and hung onto the railings, leaning back and letting his head hang and looking for the Earth, as was his habit now. He stood for a long time in this position. After a while he looked directly out at the broad lake. Underneath the bridge a long, sharp fissure had appeared in the ice and the lead-black water rose and fell against the thin rim of ice. He looked at the houses, one after the other, all the way around, and just at that moment the lights in the Parliament building came on. This heavenly silence! He stretched out his hand and saw a few flakes of snow land in the stillness and melt on his palm. He looked to the side and saw a man coming across the bridge. He was middle-aged and he was dragging his feet with difficulty through the slush. He was wearing Wellington boots and holding a bag; the Astronaut glimpsed the top of a thermos flask. He went straight up to the man and grabbed him firmly by the collar of his anorak.

"And where do you think you're going?" asked the Astronaut. "Tell me that!"

"To work, my friend," said the man.

"Shall I tell you a secret?" asked the Astronaut. Without waiting for the man to reply he said: "I'm not one of the red men, even though you may think I am." He pulled the man towards him and held him fast. "I'm not what I appear to be," he almost whispered in the man's ear. "Kaor, ha, ha, ha, I painted my face with lipstick, I was just trying to deceive you."

He made smiling grimaces at the man and waited.

"Are you sure you're feeling all right, friend?" said the man.

The Astronaut hurled the man against the railings, picked up his case, and made another circle of the lake. He met several people, but he didn't even bother to try to talk to them. He simply gave them a sidelong glance, snorted at them and pretended not to have seen them. A small aircraft came in to land, flying low over the lake. He could see there were seagulls on the ice, several hundred of them, and they rose into the air in a wave when the aircraft flew over and then settled down on the ice again.

He went back up into the Thingholt district.

He wandered about in Thingholt for a long time, every so often knocking on the walls of this house or that. There were lights on in many of the windows, the shops were open and there were increasing numbers of people around.

He was crossing a street when he remembered that Martians were able to make the old buildings of Mars fall down by the mere sound of their voices. The Astronaut put his hands to his face so as not to get splinters of glass in his eyes when the houses came crashing down, and started to make a hallowing sound as though he were gathering in sheep.

He stood hunched up and listened, keeping one hand pressed tight to his eyes.

"That's a lot of racket for so early in the morning," he heard someone say. "What's up?"

He opened his fingers and took a peep. A truck loaded with crates of beer was parked on the corner, jutting out into the street. A red-haired man in an apron was stretching to reach a crate at the back of the truck; he paused with his hand on the crate and studied the Astronaut.

Another Martian, also in an apron, came out of the shop. He stood on the steps and looked at the Astronaut with astonishment and a slight tremor of fear.

The Astronaut took his hand away from his face.

"Hey, what happened to you?"

"Nothing," said the Astronaut. "Nothing happened to me."

"Get away with you, man, no nonsense, now, what happened to you? Why have you got paint all over you, why are you that colour?"

He heard the scrunch of footsteps in the snow, and felt an arm on his shoulder. "Listen, friend," said a voice. "Don't you worry, now, we're going to have you home in a jiffy and you'll be able to have a nice lie down and rest."

Although he was in a terrible state of excitement, the Astronaut realized that the Martian must be referring to his hands, which he now saw he had forgotten to paint, and he sat down in the snow beside one of the truck's wet, dripping wheels and put his hands under his coat.

The Martians spent some time talking between themselves and then both went into the kiosk; as the Astronaut got to his feet he looked through the kiosk window and saw one of the Martians talking on the telephone. A man who ran the same kind of kiosk home on Earth came to the window and peered out inquisitively. The Astronaut ran down the street and into a side street where he concealed himself in a gateway. He put his case down on a dustbin and squatted on his heels. The house's corrugated iron was torn and rusty, and the Astronaut caught a glimpse of brown, rotten timber. The drainpipe from the roof gutter was broken in one place, and the water was gushing out. It had washed small stones from the sand against the wall of the house. The Astronaut scooped up water in his hands again and again and rubbed his face and his bald head with it for a long time. Then he trotted off with his case and caught a taxi at the next corner.

- WARLORD OF MARS -

IN ONE PLACE THE ROAD WAS BLOCKED BY A SNOWDRIFT, AND FOR A moment he was afraid they were going to arrest him and punish him for the crime, but a bulldozer appeared and cleared a way for traffic. The cabdriver turned on the radio. The sound of Icelandic came booming from it.

"Excuse me," said the Astronaut, bending right down to the set, putting his head on one side and listening; then he turned the knob and watched the station-finder move over the various cities—Helsinki, Bergen, Prague, Madrid, Milan, Tunis—making an incomprehensible symphony of voices flow from the speaker. When he came to a howling voice, he stopped turning the knob and gave the cabdriver a surreptitious glance.

"That's Turkish or some such lingo he's wailing away in, friend," said the cabdriver in a pleased tone of voice. "That's a good old radio. I've had it ever since I started to drive. That's twenty years ago now next month."

"So everything's all right back home on Terra," said the Astronaut. "I suspected as much. That's fine; I'd better be getting off home."

After the taxi had gone, he strode to and fro outside the airport terminal, not daring to go in.

Some time later a bus drew up, full of people. This was a cargo of prisoners who had fled from Earth, just as he had done, and whom the Martians were now sending home again. Open-mouthed, the Astronaut watched the people get out. He walked among them, chattering and talking nonsense with them with the greatest of pleasure, taking a look here, getting in the way there. He clapped one man firmly on the shoulder, and said: "It's great to see you, my friend. We should never ever have left home, that was a stupid thing to do. Everything's fine on Terra, I've just heard about it, but I didn't realize there were so many of us."

"They say the plane is fully booked," said the man.

I'm on my way home, thought the Astronaut as he helped to carry suitcases and accompanied the passengers inside. In his mind's eye he could see his mother's house in Reykjavik. He was looking forward to coming home. It would be good to be able to work in the kiosk again. They would probably travel at the speed of light. A short while from now he would be meeting all the people back home in Iceland and they would all be surprised to learn that each of them had his or her double on Mars.

He put on his dark glasses, found his ticket and obtained his boarding pass. A woman was standing in the doorway. "Put your case on the conveyor belt, please," she said.

"Kaor," said the Astronaut, laughing. "Why? Are you going to X-ray my black pudding and liver sausage?"

"Put you case on the conveyor belt."

"Why ?" asked the Astronaut. He put the case down, placed his right hand over his heart and made a deep bow.

"Why what?" said the woman in irritation.

"How could you have done this to us? We were just scared." He pointed to the long winding queue behind him. "I don't know about my friends here, but you ought to have realized that I don't need much room to live in."

"Done what to you?" asked the woman in bewilderment. "I've no idea what you're talking about."

"Well, well," said the Astronaut, and he laughed: "Ha, ha, ha, my dear, let's just say that it's been very nice knowing you." He gave the Martian a firm parting handshake.

He walked into an exact replica of the Freeport at Keflavik, quivering with excitement. He walked down a long passage and sat down on a stool a short distance from the bar. The only other customers seemed to be a nine-foot tall Kzin—a shaggy, reddish-yellow ape—which was standing drinking beer out of a glass, and, beside it, a three-footed puppeteer. The Kzin was evidently either saying something very funny or the puppeteer had had a few drinks too many, for every so often it drew up into a ball, fell off the barstool, took an enormous leap backwards from sheer helpless mirth, then rolled back up the same way and sat down again the right way up, saying its name out loud with an orchestral voice.

"There aren't any space-noises here. I'll have to make some for them," thought the Astronaut. And he began to sing in a high-pitched voice: "Ui, Ui, Ui, Ui, Ui, Ui."

They both looked at him and smiled shyly.

"Oh well, it's all the same to me. Let them laugh if they want to. I'm leaving Mars now, never to return." The Astronaut's mind began to turn to thoughts of home and Earth.

"Mars is a hole compared to Terra. Mars is a hole compared to Terra," he shouted over and over again, and the giant and the puppeteer stopped staring at him.

A voice over the P.A. system ordered all the passengers to board the spaceship. They walked in a long line onto the tarmac, and the Astronaut smiled faintly when he saw the jet standing illuminated in the driving snow and winter twilight. Painted on its body in large letters was the legend ICELANDAIR. His eyes grew misty. It would be good to get back home to Iceland. A Martian was attending to one of the wings.

He was lucky, and got a window seat near the back of the plane. After all that had happened during these past twenty-four hours he wanted to see Mars drop its disguise and change into the red planet.

A Japanese passenger sat down beside him. The aircraft shuddered in the high wind. The Astronaut sat with his forehead leaning on the window glass, and shortly before they flew over the sea he saw Keflavik and the airport disappear, to be replaced by the red sands and cliffs of Mars. A dark red storm was gathering on the horizon, and the clouds were turning pink. He leaned back in his seat and said to the Japanese passenger in English. "They've given up now. The sandstorms of Mars can last for months on end."

The Japanese smiled.

The Astronaut pointed skyward with his index finger and kept his hand in the air for a long time; he knew that the spaceship was leaving behind the thin atmosphere of the fourth planet. He sat up in his seat and began to survey the Earthlings on the spaceship. They seemed to be from every part of the globe. He looked at them with sympathy and affection. They'd all made the same mistake he had.

"I know how you feel," he said to the Japanese, patting him gently on the back of the hand. "I ended up in the same trouble."

Now they were approaching one of the white poles of Mars, where the warlike black men live deep inside the planet. He rang for the flight attendant, a woman.

"Excuse me," said the Astronaut, laughing nervously at the flight attendant, who was really one of the blue plant people and who didn't even notice that he'd forgotten to fasten his seatbelt. "What's that?" He pointed out of the window.

"What?"

"That pink disc over the pole."

"We're not flying that route," said the flight attendant, in a kind tone of voice. "That's the sun over the Vatnajökull Glacier. Would you like a newspaper?"

"It's the sun," said the Japanese, smiling.

"Well, thank you," said the Astronaut. "That's just fine. How long are you going to continue this tomfoolery? Do you think I don't know the sun when I see it? Whose side are you on?" he asked the Japanese. "What's going on here?"

There was a dark red disc above the expanse of ice. That wasn't the sun! No one could look at the sun without damaging his eyes. And all at once it became clear to him what was happening. The Martians had tricked him again. Why should they let him go? They weren't on their way back home to Earth as he'd thought. That black disc wasn't the sun. The sun was too far away from Mars to be as big as that. No, that was the horrifying hell-planet, Sayol, that had risen in the sky. And Sayol was the planet of no return.

He took off his dark glasses and looked around the cabin. Nobody seemed to be frightened. The Japanese had moved to another seat and was fast asleep. These weren't Earthlings who had fled from Terra, as he had supposed. They were Martians who had bought tickets so as to be able to snigger when he was turned out of the spaceship. And Sayol was a planet such that people were offered the option of having their eyes and brains removed before they were sent down to its surface. That's how they'll punish me for having killed one of them. But it was only in self-defence!

"I must get out of here," thought the Astronaut in anguish. He was really terrified now. He picked up his director's case and went to the back of the plane.

He locked himself on one of the toilets and stood there for a long time, trying to regain his wits. He looked in the mirror and observed that he hadn't made a very good job of getting rid of the lipstick—there was still a thin film of it all over his face. He tried to wash it off, but it was no good. He thought of trying to disguise himself, and picked up the lipstick, but soon thought better of the idea. It was too late for that. He opened the case, took out the axe and ran the palm of his hand along its notched blade. The axe was blunt, but its rusty head was heavy and would do the job. He peered through the opening in the door. The corridor was empty all the way to the cockpit.

Here was his chance. He would have to hijack this spaceship in the same way people hijacked airliners back home on Earth. Now he had nothing to lose. Now he could do anything. And if they refused to fly him home, he would use the axe on the instrument panel or smash their skulls open and see to it that the spaceship crashed. Nearly anything was better than Sayol.

He took hold of the shaft close up to the head, threw away his hat and strode off down the plane. In the rearmost seat sat an orange-colored Martian bird; it was resting its shiny, metal beak on the seatback behind it and was giving the earthling a sidelong stare with its red eye. "Trrrweerrll," said the man-bird. The Astronaut shook his fist at it.

He could see that a lot of the Martians were looking out of the windows and pointing, and the noise of their sniggering was overpowering. One of them turned round in his seat and laughed right in the Astronaut's face.

He strode quickly up to the pilot's cabin and opened the door without hesitation. Three of the green men were sitting at the controls dressed in full armour. One of them looked up in surprise, his protruding teeth and slimy skin gleaming.

"I want to go home," said the Astronaut. "If you don't fly me to Earth at the speed of light I'll smash the instrument panel."

"Is that all?" said the green man after he had recovered a bit. "That ought to be easy enough to arrange for you, friend."

They switched to the speed of light.

author photo by jpv

ÓLAFUR GUNNARSSON lives and works on a small farm a few miles out of Reykjavik. He published his first collection of poetry in 1970, and became a full-time writer in 1978 with the publication of his novel *Million-Percent Men*. He began a series of popular children's books with *The Beautiful Flying Whale* (1989), which received a nomination for the Nordic Children's Literature Award. He would go on to write more novels, among them the acclaimed trilogy consisting of *Troll's Cathedral* (1992), *Potter's Field* (1996), and *The Winter Journey* (1999). The English translation of *Troll's Cathedral* was nominated for the IMPAC Dublin Literature Award in 1997. In 2003, his novel *The Axe and the Earth* was awarded the Icelandic Literature Prize. Gunnarsson has also translated several works of fiction into Icelandic, including Jack Kerouac's *On the Road* and Dashiel Hammett's *The Maltese Falcon*. His most recent novel, *The Painter*, was published in 2012.